All he NEEDS

ANN GRECH

HOT TREE PUBLISHING

ALL HE NEEDS
MY TRUTH
BOOK 1

ANN GRECH

HOT TREE PUBLISHING

ALSO BY ANN GRECH

ALL HE NEEDS

IN SAFE ARMS

ALL HE NEEDS © 2019 BY ANN GRECH

All rights reserved. No part of this book may be used or reproduced in any written, electronic, recorded, or photocopied format without the express permission from the author or publisher as allowed under the terms and conditions with which it was purchased or as strictly permitted by applicable copyright law. Any unauthorized distribution, circulation or use of this text may be a direct infringement of the author's rights, and those responsible may be liable in law accordingly. Thank you for respecting the work of this author.

All He Needs is a work of fiction. All names, characters, events and places found therein are either from the author's imagination or used fictitiously. Any similarity to persons alive or dead, actual events, locations, or organizations is entirely coincidental and not intended by the author.

For information, contact the publisher, Hot Tree Publishing.

WWW.HOTTREEPUBLISHING.COM

EDITING: HOT TREE EDITING

COVER DESIGNER: BOOKSMITH DESIGN

E-BOOK ISBN: 978-1-925853-09-4

PAPERBACK: 978-1-925853-21-6

To my A-Team, this one's for you girls and guys. Thank you for loving Reef's and Ford's world as much as me, and always encouraging me to write the story Caden's been begging me to tell.

CHAPTER 1
CADEN

JUNE

The lightest of breezes whispered over my face. The fall air had a chill to it, so I was in jeans and a henley—nothing too dramatic though; Queenstown was warm compared to some of the places the world championship tour had taken me to over the past few months. I sighed, disappointment in myself coursing through my veins. Clenching my hands into fists, I tried to distract my wayward thoughts. It didn't help to think about my final season as a pro snowboarder. In one fell swoop, I'd managed to ruin my reputation, shame myself and my family, and end my career—"drug cheat" was now regularly thrown around with my name. I wasn't quite as infamous as Lance Armstrong or Ben Johnston, thank God, but yeah...

my number one claim to fame wasn't for being the five-time world champ anymore. Nope, it was my spectacular fall from grace that'd made headlines of late.

I didn't think it'd turn out this way: my life story in a nutshell. Hell, it could be the title of my autobiography. In two years I'd gone from riding the high of success to being a washed-up, banned pro athlete. My sponsors, agent, and coach had all shunned me to save their own careers. It was fair enough, but being on the receiving end of it stung.

Instead of dwelling on the past, I had to focus on the here and now, the future I could build for myself. So I shuffled forward, closer to the edge of the bridge, the yawning chasm before me. The rushing water of the Kawarau River was far below, the wooded cliffs towering high above the bridge I was standing on. The padding was strapped tight around my ankles, connected to the bridge with a long bungee cable, but it was still surreal. Looking down to the shallow river gave me the same butterflies that taking a jump on a mountain did. My heart thudded hard in my chest as a buzz sounded in my ears. Adrenaline pumped through my veins in anticipation of throwing myself off a perfectly good bridge. It was the shit I lived for.

I couldn't do it on a mountain yet—New

Zealand's ski season was still a few weeks away from starting, and I was heading home in the morning so I'd miss it anyway. I'd also been having a pity party for one. Moping about, I'd been reluctant to try anything that would give me a rush. I think I was punishing myself, but ultimately the why didn't really matter.

I'd had these grand plans of finishing out the season on a high. When I'd put feelers out, I'd had offers from a popular YouTube channel to host their snowboarding chat and highlights show within a day, and I was going to invest my sponsorship payments to give me a bit of a nest egg. But when I tested positive for a banned substance and was suspended, the offer was withdrawn. I'd felt too guilty to keep the sponsorship money I'd earned over the final year of competing, so I'd handed it back.

The future I thought I was supposed to have disappeared in a puff of smoke. Weed smoke, to be precise. It was a mistake I regretted every day since, but in that moment I just needed to relax. To sleep. I couldn't function anymore. Overwhelmed with the steaming pile of dog shit that my life had become, I'd tried everything to get a grip. Nothing had worked, so I justified to myself that smoking a joint would be okay. *What a damn idiot*. If I could go back in time, I'd bitch slap myself.

Instead, I'd been busted, and when I tried to call my agent about my options, I couldn't even get past the front desk. That's when I'd heard the line, "Michael is in meetings for the next few days. I'll have his assistant email you." I knew it was over then. I didn't even have to wait for the letter terminating my contract.

So now I had a bit of freedom, which was the only upside—if you could call a complete lack of any certainty an upside—from this clusterfuck that my life had become. Where did I want to live? I had no idea yet. Queenstown was pretty rad, and who knew, there might be a possibility, but would I really move there with my family on the other side of the world? And what the hell would I do for work? What did I *want* to do? I'd always wanted to use my hands, to be able to build something from the ground up, but would I be any good at it? Would someone even give me a go? *They* were the million-dollar questions.

The safety gate opening snapped me back to the present. The dude who'd strapped me in helped me shuffle forward. If I was going to focus on the future, I had to start now and enjoy the fuck out of this jump. I gripped the O-shaped handle to the side of the launchpad and moved my feet to the very edge. I breathed deep and smirked.

Yeah, this is gonna be fun.

"You okay, bro?" the guy in the ball cap and corporate tee asked me.

"Yeah." I grinned and nodded. "I'm good."

"Well, you can jump whenever you're ready. Usually helps to do it with a countdown."

"Eh, I live for this shit." I shrugged and pushed off the ledge, my body falling fast in a wide arc over the vast expanse. My arms outstretched on either side of me, I whooped as the pressure on my gut grew, giving me that familiar sinking feeling I'd craved since my first jump as a snowboarder. It wasn't weightlessness like skydiving, probably because I was falling headfirst, but it was a rush. It was hard to describe it, the punch to your gut when your body plummets down, freefalling into the open air. It was probably closest to the feeling I got as a kid when someone pushed me too high on a swing.

Grinning like a fool, I watched in a crazy mix of slow motion and high speed as the water drew closer and closer while I plunged down the stunningly high drop. It was about as high as some of the jumps I'd done, but it was different going down face first; I was used to being strapped to a board and having that touch the ground first. The difference between the two only heightened the experience.

I reached out, trying to touch the water, but the cord snapped me back up from a few feet away. It was then that I was weightless, being flung high into the air before falling again. That split second when I reached the peak of my ascent and began to drop again lengthened as if in slow motion, giving me the feeling of hovering, of being suspended for just the barest of moments in midair.

Two more times they let me bounce on the bungee cable before lowering me into the waiting inflatable. I laid down in the small boat and looked up at the sky as the harness around my ankles was released. Crystalline blue stretched far and wide above me, and I smiled.

Despite the shit pile that my life had turned into, it was damn good to be alive.

Once I was back in the adventure center, I collected my things from the little locker I'd put them in and headed up to catch the bus which dropped me off on the main street of Queenstown. It was only a couple of minutes until the connecting bus that would take me to my friend's house showed up. I'd only met Rick a few months earlier—Christmas in Italy, to be exact—but we'd clicked immediately. I'd traveled to the picturesque little village high in the mountains with a couple of friends—another competitor on the world championship circuit, Reef Reid, and his trainer, Mason Canning. Reef wasn't out publicly at that stage, so he was visiting his secret boyfriend, Ford, who worked alpine rescue there during the northern winter. It was the first time Mace and I had joined the celebrations that usually brought all their friends and extended family together. We were roomies for the trip, and not for the first time either. Mace always cleared out of the apartment-style hotel rooms he shared with Reef when Ford visited during the tour, wanting to give them some privacy, crashing in my room instead.

Then we'd met Riccardo, who'd returned home to Italy for the holidays, and it was as if the three of us had known each other for years. There was no other explanation except that we clicked. Now that Rick was back in New Zealand, where he lived, he'd asked Mace and me to visit. We'd both found ourselves without anywhere pressing to be, so after the season had wrapped up, we'd flown out to him. Rick lived in a big house a few minutes out of town, close to Ford's place, so the five of us—Reef and Ford included—had spent a bit of time together. But when the happy couple went home leaving the three of us together; the tension, an underlying current that ran between us, ratcheted up. I wanted to say it was sexual, but hell if I knew whether the other two felt it or if it was only in my sex-starved imagination.

It'd been far too long since I'd gotten laid, and even though I'd had a few opportunities since my season ended, I hadn't followed through, never particularly feeling it enough with anyone to get naked. I'd gone to a gay bar just before I was suspended, walked around, had one drink and then walked out. I'd Netflixed and chilled. With myself. And then I'd fallen asleep in my hotel room and dreamed of the first night Mace and I had bunked together.

"Dude, you awake?" Mace called through the closed door. *"I need somewhere to crash. Can I stay here?"*

I opened the door, half asleep and dressed only in boxers. I'd been in bed watching trash on TV. The dinner dishes still sat next to where I'd been lying, and my clothes were tossed all over the floor, my ski gear drying in front of the radiator. "Sure, but why?"

"Ford's in town, and I wanna give him and Reef some space. I've tried getting another room, but there aren't any. I know asking is kinda out there, but you're my last hope. Do you mind?"

"Nah, come on in." Letting my gaze wander down his body, I took him in from head to toe. I wanted to run my hands over his broad shoulders and down his chest to his narrow waist. He was dressed casually in sweats, but the loose material didn't do a thing to hide his physique.

When I raised my gaze again, his eyes met mine and he smiled apologetically. His light brown hair was messy, as if he'd run his fingers through the soft-looking strands. I wondered if it would be soft to the touch. Balling my hands into fists, I resisted the temptation to reach out and trace the graying patches around his temples. His beard was trimmed close and speckled with gray too, giving him that sexy sophistication that maturity brought. And he smelled good. I couldn't stop myself from breathing deep, taking his scent into my lungs.

The ever-present voice in the back of my head told me to stop, not to check him out, not to give him any hint of my orientation. I knew I could tell him—he seemed to be okay with Reef—but two of us on the tour who weren't straight? Snowboarding was hyper-masculine, and neither Reef nor I was ready to fly the pride flag. I wished I could, but really I was scared, petrified of what would happen if I came out. So I hid those parts of myself that would give me away. On top of that, Mace was straight, so there was no way in hell.

I tore my eyes away from him before my semi turned into a boner that couldn't be hidden in my state of undress.

"Thanks, C. I appreciate it. I'll…." He trailed off as he looked at the sofa.

"There's no way you'll fit on the couch." It was one of those hard, tiny ones that a kid would fit on but no one else. At six-foot-something, Mace had no hope of being comfortable.

I gulped in some air before blurting out, "If you aren't weirded out by it, you can sleep in the bed with me." Yes,

yes! *My dick cheered me on, but in my head, I knew I was screwed. I'd wanted him for years, and I knew I'd never be able to keep my hands off him—not in a sleazy way, but... well, it was more of a dirty, triple-X-rated fantasy.*

"No, that's cool." He looked at me again and smiled sheepishly, clearly embarrassed. *I wasn't sure whether it was because of his predicament, or whether he could read my thoughts. I was praying that he had no idea I'd been lusting after him for so long, but I figured I was safe—there was no way he'd volunteer to get under the sheets with me if he knew what I wanted to do to him.*

"Shit, man, I owe you one. You've literally saved my ass."

I couldn't help the bark of laughter that erupted from me. Oh, Mace, if only you knew.

Like teenage girls at a slumber party, we talked about anything and everything—where we grew up, our families, music, movies, food, our favorite holidays, everything. Well, almost everything. The one thing we avoided was snowboarding. It was as if by some unspoken agreement we knew not to speak about it. Going there could never end well for either of us. Reef was the trickiest part of our relationship. Mace was his coach. I was his competition and, I liked to think, his friend. Mace had far too much integrity to fuck any of it up. Would I have risked it for more than an innocent night with Mace? Probably not the right question to ask a drug cheat. I hadn't been busted—yet—but I had broken the rules. Smoking the joint was illegal in my sport. I just hoped I didn't get caught.

I laid awake long after he'd fallen asleep, watching his bare back rise and fall in the moonlight. My fingers itched to touch him, to reach out and stroke all that smooth, warm skin. I was bone-tired, my body exhausted from the exertion of training on the slopes all day and doing a workout that night, but my mind ran a million miles a minute, flashing glimpses at me of what I'd love to do to Mace.

I startled awake when the warm body against me shifted, pressing back into me and letting out a happy sigh. I was spooning him. I was spooning Mace.

I cracked open my eyes and, sure enough, I wasn't mistaken. It was definitely him, definitely not my imagination. I breathed in his manly smell and pressed my face into his hair, letting the strands play against my cheeks. It is as soft as I thought.

Until he woke up, I wasn't moving. I'd blame my cuddling on dreaming of a girl if I had to. Whatever it took, I was going to revel in every minute of having him in my bed, even if it wasn't real.

He ran his hand down my leg and pulled me closer to him. I was pressing my rapidly swelling cock against his ass, desperately wanting more and shying away from getting caught in that vulnerable position. There was no way I could hide my erection from him any longer; he was going to wake up and use that big hand currently wrapped around my leg to knock me the fuck out.

Then, like a ray of sunshine bursting through dark clouds and illuminating the earth below, there was a glimmer of hope. He rocked back, sliding my rigid shaft against the length of his crack. Seeing fireworks behind my closed eyelids, I used every ounce of self-restraint to stop myself from rutting against him like an animal in heat. Biting down hard on the inside of my cheek, the moan that threatened to erupt from me came out more like a whimper.

Mace subconsciously reacting that way was like a dream come true, but it didn't mean he'd appreciate another guy's cock all up in his crack in the light of day. Self-preservation had me shifting my pelvis back a sliver, but Mace mumbled something in that sleepy, sexy voice and pressed into me again before arching his back and stretching, beginning to wake up. I pulled farther away, but I couldn't let go of him completely even if I wanted to. He held my hand tight, pressing it low on his abdomen. The heat of his morning wood warmed my knuckles. God, I wanted nothing more than to sink into him and jack him off until we were a satiated puddle of goo.

Too soon, he let go of my hand and I gently slipped my arm away from him. Like the chickenshit I was, I rolled over, pretending to still be asleep. It was easier that way— he could act like it didn't happen, and I could dream of it going further without all the morning-after awkwardness.

The bus rounded a corner, the familiar road jolting me back into the present, and I huffed out a sigh, unable to deny it any longer. I was crushing on Mace. Hard. During the season, I'd secretly rejoice when Ford made his impromptu visits and he and Reef needed privacy, because then Mace would end up in my bed. I was a closeted gay guy who had a boner for his straight friend. It was clichéd enough to be a plot bunny for one of those daytime TV soap operas.

But then it got even worse. I met Rick, and for the first time in my life, I wanted to do something really insane. Way more insane than jumping off a mountain or a bridge. I wanted both of them. From the moment Mace had pushed open the door and I'd stepped into the pub on Christmas morning, I'd been riveted. The Italian god carrying lumber for the fire walked in and bent over. Seeing his windswept coal-colored hair sticking up in a spiky mess, that perfect ass and those thick thighs had my body hardening. When he'd come closer and we'd been introduced, I was hard-pressed to hide my raging boner from him. Those whiskey eyes were sharp and intelligent, and coupled with the accent, his whole look was smoking. Then he smiled and, holy shit, I nearly came in my pants.

I was hooked. On both of them.

It was almost laughable, wanting not one but two men. Even if they swung that way, I wasn't exactly the picture of integrity, the boy you'd take home to meet Mom and Dad. And the two of them deserved that, to fall for someone who was worth more than a back-alley fuck. I was rushed blow jobs in club bathrooms, the hookup in someone's truck with a minor celebrity, while they were fairy tales and romance.

But none of that stopped my traitorous mind imagining myself between them, or my dick getting hard when I watched them laugh together while we cooked dinner or hung out relaxing after Rick finished work for the day. And hey, in Caden's world of make-believe, we'd be happy and in love and it'd all be rainbows and unicorns.

Hell, Ford's cousin Connor had a boyfriend *and* a girlfriend. It wasn't completely impossible, and even if it was, I could dream.

Right?

CHAPTER 2
CADEN

The bus stopped and I climbed off, stepping down onto the gravel beside the road, breathing in the crisp air as I took in the view of the Remarkables. The towering mountains stood over me like a sentinel watching over the land, the snow hanging low on the slopes, promising a good season. I would love to stay there for the winter, but it wasn't in the cards. My sister's baby wasn't going to wait, and I'd promised to be there for the birth; her baby daddy wasn't around, and I couldn't let her go through labor alone. But I was reluctant to leave. Queenstown called to me, and I liked it here, but I was fast running out of time. I would be on a flight home—well, to my sister's home in Florida—early the next morning.

On a whim, I decided to stop in at Reef and Ford's house on my way to Rick's, unsure whether

I'd see them again for a while. Voices carried on the breeze to me as I turned the corner one house away from Ford's, and I heard his familiar British accent from the front yard. I couldn't see him yet, the neighbor's hedge was in the way, so I quickened my pace to catch him and Reef before they went inside or left. But when I heard what Ford said, I hesitated. It sounded like a private conversation, and I didn't want to intrude.

"Mace, listen to me. Tell him. Be straight with him. There's no other way."

"He's gonna hate me, and I don't want to lose him."

Don't want to lose who? My footsteps faltered. I didn't want to eavesdrop, but if Mace was upset, I wanted to be there to help. My promise to my sister wasn't an obligation for me—I couldn't wait to meet my niece or nephew, but Mace had done so much for me without even realizing it. I was torn, loyalty to my friends and family pulling me to opposite parts of the globe.

"Mace—" That time it was Reef who spoke, his tone confident but full of warning.

"I know, I'm being selfish." There was a pause. I couldn't see Mace bite his bottom lip, but I pictured him doing it. His nervous habit always revved me up, but that time my libido wasn't raring to go. My gut was telling me that something was off. "I'm scared, all right? I ended his career, for fuck's sake."

I sucked in a sharp breath, a bucket of ice-cold water dousing me. Dread settled over me like a heavy fog, chilling me to my bones. We were supposed to be friends. I couldn't lose that. I couldn't lose him. Disbelief and anger warred within me, but a tiny ray of hope shined too. Until I heard my name, there was a chance it was someone else. Wasn't there? Maybe?

Please let me be wrong. Please, not Mace.

"Caden's important to me, and I screwed it up. He'll never forgive me, and now I can't even man up and tell him. I should've sat him down as soon as it happened, before I even reported it, but I'm a chickenshit. Now he's leaving again, and I've waited too long. If I tell him tonight, he'll walk away and I'll never have the chance to fix it."

My hope shattered, leaving a great gaping void in its place. Like melting snow trickling down the mountain in spring, anger slowly filled me. *What the fuck has he done?*

Reef spoke again. "He'll be pissed, yeah, but what's the alternative? Don't tell him? Let him go home clueless?"

Ford continued on, like he was finishing his partner's thoughts for him. "The drug test wasn't random, and it's not fair to Caden to let him keep thinking it was. You did your job and reported him. It sucks, but he needs to know."

I couldn't listen anymore. Rage bubbled inside me. He'd deceived me, kept a secret that'd destroyed everything I'd worked for. The only thing I could think was why? Why Mace? Why did he do it? Why would he hurt me like that? He'd betrayed me.

Angry tears sprang to my eyes and I scrubbed them away, furious with myself for letting my emotions show. He'd known I was struggling. He knew what a toll Mom's death had taken on me, and yet he'd used my private battle to break me. All those moments between us—our entire friendship, the trust I placed in him—crumbled before my eyes, shattering into a million pieces like my heart was.

Unlike so many others, I thought Mace had stuck with me when the shit with the World Anti-Doping Agency had gone down, but he'd been the one to cause it. Was he getting off on seeing me struggle and flounder? Or was he guilty?

Then it hit me. How long had Reef and Ford known? Were they all in on it? I'd been surrounded by yes-men since I'd made it big. Everyone wanted something from me, but I thought I'd found some true friends; people who liked me for me. In Mace, I thought I'd found someone who didn't care whether

I won or lost, whether I was even on the pro tour. But that wasn't the case at all. He'd led me on, betrayed me, and now I had no one. There wasn't anyone left I could trust.

Loneliness stabbed through me. The others—my coach, my agent, those "friends" who'd left me in their wake—I could handle, but knowing it was Mace who'd called in the drug testers cut deep.

I stepped out from behind the hedge and stopped in front of Ford's house. There they were, standing in the drive only a few feet away from me. Mace looked up, the color draining from his face when my eyes locked with his hazels. I didn't say a word to him. I couldn't. Instead, I shook my head and kept walking.

"C," he called. When I didn't answer, he shouted out to me again, his footsteps crunching on the gravel after me.

"Save it, Mace." My voice was raw, filled with the emotions I was trying to hold back. I wanted to say so much more, but I couldn't get the words out without showing him just how hurt I was.

"Lemme explain," he begged, grabbing my arm. I didn't turn. I wouldn't give him the satisfaction of knowing he'd broken a piece of me that I didn't think I could ever get back. His whispered "Please" had me clenching my jaw and shaking my head.

I pulled out of his grasp and muttered the only

word I could. "No." One step and then another put enough distance between us that I couldn't feel the heat radiating off his body anymore. Each breath I took was like a sharp knife twisting in my chest, and I struggled with each inhale.

Then I ran.

It wasn't until I'd closed Rick's front door and was in the safety of his living room that I could breathe again. The silence in the house was cloying, and I'd barely made it up the stairs and into the bedroom I was staying in before I was itching to leave again. There was no way I was sticking around waiting for Mace to get there. Rick would understand if I left earlier than expected. Maybe.

I powered up my tablet, clicking on the airline's link. The sooner I got out of Queenstown, the better. I wouldn't be able to change my international flight, but at least if I got away, I wouldn't have to see Mace again.

I had three hours until my flight to Auckland left. My Uber was on the way, and I just had a few more things to throw into my pack.

The door banged open and I heard my name on Mace's lips. I'd fantasized about having that mouth say my name in an entirely different way, but no more. Shoving the last of my stuff in my bag, I zipped it and hauled it onto my shoulders just as Mace walked into my room.

"Please let me explain," he murmured. He was hurting, it was obvious, but I couldn't deal. I had to get out of there.

"There's nothing *to* explain, Mace." I pushed past him and walked away. It took all my strength to do it, to leave him standing there while anger, hurt, and betrayal coursed through me. I never expected it to be something I'd do.

I was torn. I wanted to tell him to go to hell, but at the same time beg him to explain why.

The stairs were interminably long, but I finally reached the front door. I paused, my hand on the knob, feeling the weight of his stare against the back of my head. There was more we both needed to say, but I couldn't. Not then. Maybe one day, when the dust settled and the gaping wound in my chest wasn't so raw, I'd be able to face him again.

"Caden," he begged.

I leaned my forehead against the door and blew out a breath. Damn, it hurt.

"Goodbye, Mace."

Opening the door, I stepped out into the late afternoon air and shivered. I was cold down to my bones, almost numb with it. Closing the door behind me was hard, but seeing Rick in the drive looking at me with confusion nearly broke me. I didn't want to leave, not like this, but what choice did I have?

"You were gonna leave without saying goodbye?" Rick's voice, deep and smooth like caramel and whiskey—the perfect match to his eyes—spoken in that sexy-as-fuck Italian accent, settled over me. I hadn't seen him in his helicopter pilot's uniform before. The olive coveralls wouldn't be flattering on most people, but it highlighted his broad shoulders and narrow waist. In it, he stole my breath. Something else I couldn't deal with in that moment.

"I didn't want to, Rick, but...." I trailed off, unable to finish the sentence. It hit me then—I had no idea whether I'd ever see him again. Leaving wasn't temporary this time. I didn't have a job, didn't have any real friends. Who knew what I'd end up doing and where it'd be.

"He told you, didn't he?"

My gaze shot up to meet his once more, and I saw sadness in his eyes. The words I wanted to say stuck in my throat. Rick stepped up to me and gave me an awkward hug, my pack getting in the way. My arms wound around his wide back and I clutched tight. His warmth, his strength, wrapped around me, and I breathed deep. He smelled good, something spicy and exotic, something I'd never forget.

"I'm sorry you're hurting." Pulling back, he looked me in the eye. His lips were turned down, his normally bright eyes dull. He looked broken, exactly like me. My leaving was hurting him too. "I understand why you need to get away, but your time here isn't over. Once your sister and her baby are settled, come back and stay with me. You can make a home here. You could be happy."

"You'd want me back in your space again? Even with my socks lying around all over the place?" I teased, trying to lighten the boulder in my stomach. This was the goodbye I wasn't ready for.

"What socks?" He smiled and kissed my cheek softly. To everyone else, he kissed both cheeks in that ridiculously charming and uniquely European way, but I received one lingering one and I loved it. "See you in three months. No longer, *sì?*"

"I'll try." I nodded and stepped away, trying but failing to smile. "Bye, Rick. Thanks for everything." I had to turn away, and when I did, I saw Mace standing in the doorway, looking just as defeated as I felt.

Whatever. It was his fucking fault.

The wall of Florida heat and humidity hit me hard when I stepped out of the airport. It was already hot, even for spring. I looked around, squinting in the bright sun. It didn't take me long to see my sister's bright red Jeep—her pride and joy, which she'd named George—parked in the pick-up zone with the trunk open. Annalise leaned against it, her swollen belly stretching her Army T-shirt to the max.

I waved and moved over to her, watching her casually flip her keys over in her hand. The armed airport policeman who was knocking on car windows making people move off walked around her. She tipped her head at him in acknowledgment and smirked at me. Annalise was a badass, and even though she was about to pop, no one would be stupid enough to mess with her. Years of training in explosive ordinance disposal with the Army made her lethal. Literally. She could blow you into a million pieces in her sleep.

"Hey, you. Welcome home." Annalise smiled and hugged me tight, her grip strong. I held her longer than she was probably comfortable with, but I'd missed her and truth be told, I was still smarting from Mace's news. Leaving early hadn't helped; it'd just given me a lot of uncomfortable hours to wait in an airport lounge with nothing to do except ruminate on the whys.

But enough of that. I was home—well, at my sister's house anyway. My hometown was a long way away from there. Dad had sold everything when Mom died and moved into Annalise's. He couldn't handle the memories, and my sister had been expecting to deploy, so he was going to house-sit for her. When her authorization to deploy was pulled because of her pregnancy, Dad stayed. Now there were going to be four of us living together, but at least I'd be with my favorite person in the world.

I tossed my pack in the trunk and slammed it shut before turning to her. "Look at you, snotface. You're huge." I couldn't help the grin I gave her, chuckling at her angry stare from my teasing. "Whale-sized, even."

I knew it was coming, but it still stung when she punched me in the arm. Figuring I might as well push my luck, I held out my hand for the keys.

Annalise raised her eyebrows and just stared, daring me to piss her off.

"You shouldn't be driving," I told her with as straight a face as possible. "Seriously, women in your condition should really just be preparing for the baby. Resting and, you know, washing and folding those cute little clothes. You're too fragile in your state. *Way* too emotional too."

My sister stepped up to me, her belly bumping

my flat one. She'd squared her shoulders and looked like she was priming for a fight, but her eyes danced with humor. "Do you want me to castrate you? Because *seriously*, I could do it with my keys. My blunt, rusty keys."

"Is there a problem here, ma'am?" the police officer from earlier asked, stepping into our line of sight. I bit back my laugh, unable to suppress my grin.

Annalise smiled sweetly at him and batted her eyes before saying, "No, sir, my brother's just asking to get his ass kicked. He called me fat and told me I was too fragile to drive."

The dude's eyes bugged out and he stuttered before looking at me, horrified. I couldn't help laughing then. My heart was lighter than it had been in a long time. *I should've come home instead of going to Queenstown. What was I thinking?* Hoping I could turn friendship into something more—especially when one of them was built upon a lie—was ridiculous.

I wrapped my arm around her neck, rubbing my knuckles over her hair. It was pulled back in a slick bun, and she'd really be pissed at me if there were any strands out of place. Even on leave, she was still so obviously military. "You're beautiful, Anna. No matter how whale-like you look." I let go of her and stepped away before she could elbow me in the nuts.

"Thanks for picking me up. And you do look beautiful. You always do."

"Get in, idiot balls." It was her nickname for me from when she was twelve, and hearing it again made me smile. I stepped forward again and kissed her hair before walking around and opening the driver door for her, closing it when she'd taken a seat.

Snapping on my belt, I grinned at her as she pulled into traffic, the growl of the powerful engine impressive. We caught up on the little things as she made the short trip to her home. Seeing it again made me cringe and excited at the same time. The house was run down, the paint peeling, the siding broken in places, and the stairs sagged too. It had good bones, but it was obvious that the landlord hadn't given it any love. It had so much potential, if only someone made an effort to fix it up. I half wondered why Dad hadn't done anything, but I knew he hadn't been coping.

It took a moment, but I saw him sitting in exactly the spot Annalise described—a seat in the shade of the big orange tree in the yard. He didn't acknowledge us pulling up, just stared out to space in his own world.

Anna saw my concern, murmuring quietly to me when she'd come around to the back of George.

"He's been there all morning. The only thing he does is fish from his boat or on the dock, sit there, or sleep. I have to force him to eat some days." Elbowing me in the side, she smiled, lightening the mood. "Hey, you just got to put your junk in George's trunk. How'd it feel to get lucky?"

I cracked a grin and shook my head. "You're insane. You know that, don't you?" I pulled my bag out of the car and swung it over my shoulder. "And it wasn't nearly as satisfying as putting my junk in a trunk should feel."

She and Dad both knew I was gay. Apart from my hookups, who I only ever used my middle name with, they were the only two people alive who I'd confided in.

I pushed the thought aside. It wasn't a big deal anymore. I wasn't a pro snowboarder, and I didn't have the spotlight on me either. The media circus had ended a while ago, thankfully, and because no one knew me here, maybe I'd be able to get out and have some fun.

I squashed that thought as quickly as I had it. I was there for Annalise and the baby, not to get laid.

Anna headed inside and I wandered over to Dad. It wasn't until I stood right in front of him that he looked up, suddenly realizing that he wasn't alone.

"Caden," he said, sounding surprised. "Sorry, I

was a world away. Welcome home, son."

"Thanks, Dad. It was a long flight. I'm glad to finally be here."

It was awkward speaking with him. Mom's death had broken him; now he was a shadow of the strong, vibrant man he used to be, and I ached knowing the pain he lived with every day.

"Go inside and rest up. Maybe we can go out to eat tonight instead of your sister cooking. My treat."

I scowled. "You should be helping her, not leaving everything up to Anna to do. She's ready to have this baby any day now, and you know her—she won't ask for help."

Annalise wandered over to us then, and I bit back the rest of my lecture, shaking my head at him. "I've got some sweet tea inside." She motioned up the stairs with her thumb. "Go relax."

"I need a shower." I pulled my funky-ass shirt away from my damp skin. "Then I'm gonna look around and see what needs to be done to the house to make it safe for you." I stared pointedly at Dad, but he was staring off into space again.

She nodded and glanced at her watch. "I have a checkup with the doc on base in an hour. I'm booked in next week so... yeah." She grinned, obviously happy but also nervous.

"Ah." I was suddenly speechless. It was really

going to happen. I was going to be an uncle. I grinned, happiness sending my gut into cartwheels. *So freaking cool.* "Is he still breech?"

"She—"

"He."

With a smirk on her face, she continued. "Yes, *the baby's* still breech. It's gonna be a C-section delivery."

Talking about the baby made excitement vibrate off her. The thought of someone cutting me open to extract a living creature scared the shit out of me, but then again, pushing it out of a hole that I was sure wasn't meant for watermelon-sized objects was probably worse. I don't know how many times I'd thought I was happy to be a man after looking at the baby websites Anna had sent me links to. "I'll finally get to meet her."

"I can't wait." I wrapped my arm around her shoulders and squeezed. "Will the doc still let me stay with you?"

"Absolutely. You're my moral support."

DAD INSISTED ON GOING OUT, AND ALTHOUGH I WAS dubious about the diner he'd chosen, the chicken fried steak and biscuits were the best I'd ever had. We all retired to bed early after supper, and I laid in my room, my body spent. The change in time zones had knocked me around, and if it weren't for the stairs I had to replace, and the stiff windows I needed to look at the next day, I could have slept for a week.

My emotions were all over the place too. Maybe it was just because I was so tired, but Mace's text from earlier had me wanting to throw my cell out the car window.

Hope your flight was good. Figured you'd be there by now. I know it's not the time, but I'd really like to talk. Maybe when you can, call me. Or I can call you, whatever works. I don't wanna lose you.

I was pissed at him, but my gut flip-flopped just seeing his name on my screen. I couldn't bring myself to respond though, so I'd closed the message and pocketed my cell. Now it was eating away at me. The reminder that I hadn't responded, taunting me.

Scrubbing a hand over my face, I let my eyes drift closed and a familiar face flashed in my mind's eye. *Mom.* My mood slipped. I still couldn't smile when I thought of her, even though I had so many amazing memories growing up. Mom dying was still too raw, her loss still so shocking that the air would be sucked out of my lungs whenever I thought about how quickly she'd been taken from us. The cancer had been diagnosed as a fast-growing malignant tumor in her right breast, but it'd quickly spread throughout her body. Chemo and radiation therapy after the operation to remove the cancer hadn't worked, and four months later, instead of celebrating her birthday, we'd buried her. Now whenever I thought of her, I saw Mom's sleeping form as death took her.

Fuck you, cancer. Fuck. You.

That was why I had been such a basket case for so long. My nights were filled with reliving the moment Mom let out that final exhale, her body going still and the silence surrounding her becoming deafening. Annalise and Dad had held her in those last few moments, tears tracking down their faces. Me? I'd been on the other side of the room, as far away from her as I could be because I was too scared to touch her. She'd been in so much pain, and her pale skin and emaciated frame looked so frail that I hadn't wanted to add to her agony, especially in those final days.

The guilt of somehow depriving her of a moment she might've needed haunted me. I hated that I was too much of a coward to comfort her. Now that I couldn't see her again, I knew I shouldn't have been so selfish. I hated myself for the heartbreak I caused her. Didn't matter that I hadn't meant to hurt her;

she'd needed me to comfort her, and I'd failed. I didn't have a defense other than I was stupid. I saw how she writhed in pain, how she gasped for air because it hurt her so much to even breathe that she would almost pass out. I justified my selfish cowardice with compassion for her. And now I lived with the knowledge that I'd distanced myself while being in the same room as her when she took her last breaths.

Was I distancing myself again with Mace? Was I trying to protect myself and hurting him instead? *No. Fuck him, he deserves it. Why should I worry about hurting him when he took everything from me?*

But that wasn't true either. I'd done it to myself. I only had myself to blame. When I'd been competing, the guilt, the knowledge that the last memory my mother had of me was hurting her, made me want to destroy myself, to throw everything away and drop off the face of the earth, but I couldn't do it. The competitive streak in me had my balls in a vise grip and wouldn't let go. The season was grueling in and of itself, but the added layers of grief, self-contempt and drive to succeed against all odds had made the tour impossible to bear. I was desperate for a few solid hours of uninterrupted sleep, and I was so strung out that insanity was a real possibility. So I'd justified cheating to myself.

Nothing else is working, Caden. It's not like you're using steroids. Weed isn't performance enhancing; it'll just relax you a bit. You'll never finish the season if you don't get a grip. Imagine how proud Mom would be if you finished on top and could dedicate the win to her.

Thing was, the weed *was* performance enhancing. I was cracking under the pressure, riding on adrenaline alone, and my scores were dropping. Then I'd smoked a joint and had a decent meal and a few hours of sleep that were so deep, not even my nightmares could invade them. And bam! I was competitive again. I beat Reef in a few of the heats, and I was making everyone around me happy once more. It was good to please them, to have Dan, my coach, smile at me when I left the slope rather than growling.

It hadn't helped that Dan and I weren't getting along for other reasons too. I'd always been the life of the party, out until late, surrounded by a mob of snow bunnies. I'd never corrected any of the ridiculous stories about my sex life. According to the rumor mill, I took a new girl home with me every night, sometimes two. Truth was, I'd walked many a too-drunk girl back to her hotel and made out with her in the lobby to fuel the stories on social media, then rode up to her room, dropped her off and escaped out of the hotel via a different door. After all, it was easy to hide that I was gay when everybody assumed I'd been with more women than you could count. I even stooped to playing dumb a few times when I could see people getting too close to the truth about me. I'd asked Reef a few stupid questions when he saw me staring at Mace one time. They were ones I damn well knew the answer to, but they were favorites of the ignorant straight community: "What do you do with two dicks?" and "Don't you miss the curves and softness?"

I might've tried to do the right thing by drunk girls, but Dan was another story. He'd take advantage—literally—of every one of the snow bunnies I tried to let down nicely. It made me the ultimate wingman without even trying. He got lucky with at least one of the women I'd refuse every night. But when I stopped going out as often, struggling to come to terms with my guilt and loss, it put a serious dent in his sex life. If there was one thing I'd learned from living in close quarters with my coach, it was that he was a bear when he was horny.

Dan was so keen to get me back up to peak performance—in the bars, not on the slopes—that he'd lined me up to try every natural remedy out there to get me back on an even keel. Whatever was permitted by the World Anti-Doping Agency—meditation, yoga, acupuncture, massage, hot tubs, orgasms, approved anxiety meds, everything—he had me try. He'd joked one time that his dick had a vested interest in me being happy and well-rested again. Not him, not his reputation, not his interest in me as his long-time mentee. His dick.

It hurt, but I dutifully tried everything he lined up, and none of it worked. Even the hooker with the double D's walked away dissatisfied. So I did shit my way and smoked a joint. I managed to pass the first drug test—the THC must've been out of my system when I pissed in the cup—but I wasn't so lucky with the second one. I'd known it was coming, but it still stung when I was pulled aside after my final run of the season—the championship event that could've seen me beat Reef—only to be given the positive test results and the official suspension by the governing body.

I sighed and kicked off the sheet. The overhead fan squeaked, but there was no way I was turning it off; the breeze coming in from the open window was cool, but not cool enough. I picked up my cell, flipping it in my hands in the darkness. *Should I? Shouldn't I?* Finally, I gave in and brought up Rick's contact, hitting *Call* before I could change my mind.

It'd barely rung at my end before he answered. I could hear the smile in his voice as he greeted me warmly and asked, "You made it okay? Your sister good?"

"Yeah, I did. Anna looks great. She's feisty and excited. I really missed her. I feel bad that I spent so long away even after the season ended. I should've been here more for her. The house is falling apart, and Dad's been no help." I sighed. "He's not coping, and Anna's had to look after him as well as herself." I scrubbed my hand over my face. "Sorry to unload on you, man. You don't wanna hear about my crap."

"Yes I do. Talk to me. I've got time."

So I did. I talked about what was urgent on the house and what help Annalise needed to get set up before the baby came. Rick's encouragement steeled my resolve and had me mentally planning what I'd start with. The more I talked to him, the more I knew I could handle things. He gave me hope. He made me want to be brave.

"You sound like you've made up your mind on where you want to be. That's good, Caden. I'm happy you've got that."

His words struck me like a wrecking ball. I did want to stay and help Anna raise the baby, something I didn't even know I wanted until he'd said it. I didn't even know who the baby daddy was, and I wanted to take on the part for my niece or nephew. I wanted to see them grow up, teach them and read them bedtime stories. Annalise would go on deployment eventually too—it was inevitable—and I wanted to be there then and always.

"I do. But that means not coming back to Queenstown."

A heavy weight settled in my chest, like I knew I was going to miss out on something spectacular if I didn't go back. And it wasn't just the ski season. I was being drawn there, pulled by some unseen force, except that I wasn't so sure it was unseen. It was Rick. And before Mace had turned out to be such an asshole, it was him too.

"If we're meant to see each other again, we will," he assured me. "I don't give up easily, and I hope you don't either. We'll find a way." I closed my eyes and let his words wash over me, soothing me. *We'll find a way.* "Good night, Caden. Sleep well."

"Good night, Rick," I whispered, my voice already thickening with sleep. Hanging up, I clutched my cell and rolled to my side, relaxing into the pillow.

I knew what I needed to do in the morning, a trip to the lumberyard first on the list. I had purpose, something I hadn't had a lot of since I'd found myself at the end of my professional career, and I had Rick to thank for encouraging me.

I smiled into the darkness and let sleep take me.

CHAPTER 3
CADEN

"Will you answer his text, please?" Annalise gave me the stink eye over the glass she was drinking from. "You've been studying your cell for a week like it's holding the key to finding Atlantis."

I shook my head and put down the roasting dish I'd pulled out of the oven, dropping in the potatoes I'd just peeled and sliding it back in. "I'm not sure I'm ready to, Anna. I can't help but feel like Mace betrayed me. He's texting me, begging me to let him explain, but if he was a true friend, he would've talked to me before he fucking tattled on me."

"Listen to me, Caden. Life is short. One minute you're here, and the next you could be gone." I knew she was talking about Mom and more than one of her Army buddies who hadn't made it back from a tour. For someone her age, she was far too experienced with death. "You have to live every moment. Don't waste even a single minute. You can't hold on to grudges. It just makes you bitter. Forgive him and move on, not for him but for you."

"How is forgiving him good for me?"

She looked at me like I was stupid and huffed out a breath. "Before you found out, how would you have described him? Not his looks, his personality."

"Loyal and fun. He's a good guy, a decent man, you know? But I've had to rethink everything I thought I knew. A decent guy doesn't rat out his friends."

"You're my big brother, and I love you, but you really are dumb sometimes. Do you know what makes a good man? A decent man?" She didn't let me get an answer in even if I'd tried. "Doing the right thing. If he'd asked you point-blank whether you were doing drugs, what would you have said? Would you have lied to save your ass, or would you have trusted him to keep a secret that proved you were acting illegally? Don't you think that by him going to the Anti-Doping Agency, he gave you the best chance? If you were clean, you would've passed the test no problems. If not, well…"

"You don't think I deserved to be in contention for the championship, do you?" I challenged. I knew

I was being overly defensive, but how was I supposed to react? "You're gonna side with him?"

"I'll always be on your side, you know that. But that doesn't mean you did the right thing. You now have the chance to become a better man, and a better man would call his friend and talk it through."

"Yeah, yeah," I dismissed her.

"You're upset because you care about him. Don't let this become a regret." She squeezed my arm and kissed me on the cheek before walking out.

I sagged against the kitchen countertop, all the fight going out of me. She was right like always.

Scrubbing my hand over my cheek, I let out a heavy breath. I needed to call him. *I'll do it tonight.* I'd call him when the others went to bed and I could have a decent conversation with him without my sister listening in.

I still had to rehang all of the pictures in Anna's room after I'd repainted it, and I wanted to get the stain on the front steps down too. I'd worked like the possessed since I'd been back, getting everything urgent fixed up. All the windows in the house now opened easily and were freshly painted, the loose kitchen cupboard doors were screwed tight again and the stairs were brand new. The house already looked better, and with a fresh coat of paint outside, it'd no longer be the worst house on the street.

It was well past suppertime before I finished everything. After a shower, I fell into bed, my eyes closing as soon as I laid my head on the pillow.

No. I have to call Mace.

Rousing myself, I grabbed my cell and brought up his contact before I could talk myself out of it again. I was disappointed when it went straight to his message service, and that was a first. I didn't think I'd ever want to speak with him again. Anna was right, forgiving him did lighten the weight I'd been carrying. I didn't bother leaving a message for him, knowing he hardly ever listened to them, and fired off a text instead.

> **Hey, Mace. Tried calling, but you can see that. I'm gonna get some sleep now, but I'll call tomorrow after Anna has the baby. I'm gonna be an uncle. Cool, huh? We've both got some stuff to say, so we should talk.**

I didn't get a response before I fell asleep, but that was probably a good thing.

In less than twenty-four hours, my life would be changed forever. I'd be holding a baby in my arms—a boy, with any luck—while my sister recovered.

Excitement rippled through me, sparking like the striking of a match. I couldn't wait.

"Hello, Mom." A man in scrubs pulled one side of the peach-colored curtain across the opening before holding out his hand to shake Annalise's over her belly. With a smile, he turned to me. "I'm Dr. John Cleary, your anesthetist. You must be Caden. It's a pleasure to meet you."

After shaking my hand, he perched himself on the end of the bed Annalise was sitting on. "Okay, let's go through the information you gave me last time we met so we're all on the same page. Then I'll put in the cannula and give you something for the nerves."

I looked around the ward while they spoke, taking in the white walls and the beige linoleum flooring, the muted watercolors of landscapes hanging on the walls. It was all very calming, so different from the swanky private respite center Mom died in. The contrast was a relief. The thought of going somewhere like that again had me waking up in a cold sweat the night before.

"Okay, let's do this."

I turned at his words to see the doctor pull open a packet with a giant needle in it. I was morbidly curious, dying to watch my sister's reaction. She hated needles. Abso-fucking-lutely hated them. It sounded callous, me getting a kick out of my sister's fears, but at least she was fearful of something you rarely came across. Me? I had a stupid, irrational fear of birds. Hated the bastards with a passion. It wasn't fun growing up—she took every chance to tease the ever-loving shit out of me.

"Out," Anna ordered, pointing to the privacy curtain.

I pouted playfully but made my exit all the same and stood on the other side of the drapes. Anna hissed at what I assumed was the pinch, and instead of being disappointed, I was proud of her for being so damn brave. Lord knew I hadn't overcome my fear.

I tentatively poked my head back in just as the doc said we'd be going through to the operating room in twenty minutes. My pulse leaped, but that time in a good way.

I grinned at Anna. "It'll be on like *Donkey Kong*."

"It's time to kick ass and chew bubblegum," she replied, impersonating *Duke Nukem* in a weirdly accurate way.

Annalise and I were taken through exactly twenty minutes later. Once she was settled, I held her hand and resolutely looked at the walls while the anesthetist jabbed her in the back with another needle. Apparently, that one blocked all the pain so she could have the cesarean. It was all a little overwhelming, but Anna was taking it in stride and still ordering me around. She had a plan of exactly what she wanted to do after the baby was born: chest-to-chest cuddling and breastfeeding for the colostrum, but bottle feeding after that. I hadn't even known what colostrum was until two days ago, so I was happy to go with the flow.

Helping her lie down, I resisted the urge to crack another joke about her being a beached whale, not wanting to risk being stabbed in the eye by one of the stainless-steel instruments on the tray near me. Still, I couldn't help my smirk, and even though the words weren't spoken, Anna glared at me, almost daring me to open my mouth.

Once she was comfortable, the nurses laid a sheet over her, and I undid the tie at the back of her neck so she could slip off the gown when ready to feed the baby. The nurses dropped the green sheets down so they acted as a dividing wall between Anna's face and her belly. It extended out far enough that I couldn't see anything either, thank God. I was her support person, but there was no way I could watch the operation. Then again, doing it by C-section would surely be better than going through hours of screaming. If I were a straight dude and on the business end of a delivery, I don't think I'd ever look at pussy the same again.

I bit back a laugh and Anna shook her head, grinning at me. "I know that look. What are you laughing about?"

"I'm thinking that I'm grateful I'm not a straight guy who has to see his wife's bits being mangled by a baby, because I dunno if I'd wanna be all up in that any time soon after the birth."

Anna laughed, as did the anesthetist.

"Trust me, Mr. Lambert, no woman would want you all up in her bits any time soon after the birth either. That feeling is entirely mutual," an older woman in green scrubs, a face mask, and white latex gloves said as she moved the implements on the tray around. "Hello, Annalise. Great seeing you again."

"You too, Helen."

I was introduced to Anna's doctor while she connected Annalise to a bunch of machines. Then Helen gave us a rundown of exactly what would happen from there on out. It wouldn't take long for the delivery, and after Annalise was looked after and the baby had latched on properly for a feed, we'd all be transferred back to the ward. Anna didn't want the baby to go into the nursery, so a little cot was going to be brought in with us.

Excitement buzzed in the air between us, both of us giddy. It was nothing like I'd ever experienced before. I'd been on some big stages, had performed at the heights of my sport, even stood on the podium after winning gold at the Olympics, but it was nothing compared to this. Knowing a new life was being brought into the world in a moment's time was surreal, absolutely brilliant. I suddenly understood why characters broke out into song during all the happy parts in a Disney movie.

I ran my fingers through my sister's hair and smiled down at her, planting a kiss on her forehead. "This is it, huh? You'll do great, snotface. You're gonna be the best mom around." Taking her hand in mine, I added, "I can't wait to meet him."

"Her." Anna grinned and squeezed my hand, becoming more serious for a moment. "Thank you for being here, *idiot balls*."

"I wouldn't be anywhere else." I ran my fingers through her hair again, mainly to keep my hands busy. I hated not being able to do anything, having to just sit there while the doctors did their work. Annalise wasn't in pain, she was comfortable and joyful, but I still wanted to be more than the token dude who held her hand. Looking at her, I could see the excited sparkle in her green eyes. Her smile was wide. I'd never seen her happier.

Before I knew it, the doctors were telling her that the baby was out. They were cutting the cord, about to hand the baby over so Anna could see for herself whether she'd had a boy or girl.

My excitement had fizzled though, my concentration snagging on Annalise. Something had changed in her—a tiny frown replacing the smile, the color fading from her face. Machines started beeping, alarms sounding as the anesthetist called out, "BP's dropping."

"Anna," I called out, my voice shaking. "Anna, talk to me." I was loud, too loud with a new baby in the room, but fear shot through me.

"I'm dizzy," she whispered, reaching up to press her fingertips against the bridge of her nose. Her arm went limp midair, dropping by her side and hanging off the table as her eyes rolled back in her head. All the air rushed out of my lungs, and I lunged to grasp her hand again. Holding it in my own, I squeezed, but she didn't squeeze back.

Confusion swirled around me. *I don't understand. Why isn't she squeezing my hand anymore?* "Anna," I begged. *What's wrong with her? Why isn't she answering?* "Anna." I looked around, frantic for someone to *do* something.

"Help her!" My shout cut through the chaos, but no one stopped moving as they spoke in a language I didn't understand. Monitors and sirens blared around me, and over it all, I heard the cries of a tiny baby.

Anna's baby.

"Get him out," the doctor ordered. "Now."

Fuck no. I'm not going anywhere.

The nurse closest to me took me by the arm and tried to lead me out, but I shook her off. I couldn't leave Anna. I needed to help her, but the more I fought, the harder I tried, the further she slipped, like a chasm was opening and separating us. I watched on, desperate to stop her slide.

Annalise's lips were turning blue.

No.

That shouldn't happen. It wasn't supposed to happen.

Desperate, I shook her, trying to wake her up. "Wake up, Anna," I cried. "Please." I was begging, tears springing to my eyes.

She wasn't answering. She wasn't waking up.

Arms hooked around my middle, dragging me away. No matter how hard I fought, the arms around me were stronger.

"Anna!" I shouted.

Flailing, I was practically lifted and carried out. I threw my hands out, trying to grasp on to something to stop my exit, but I met nothing but air until my fingertips brushed against the frame of the door. Instinctively, I curled my hands around the ledge and held on, using every ounce of strength I possessed.

Not letting go. Not leaving. I can't abandon her. I need to stay. I have to help her.

Then I saw the blood, and my own went cold. Blood was everywhere. Anna, the curtain, the doctor —they were covered. It was pooling on the floor and growing bigger, spreading wider. Footprints were being tracked around the room by the nurses rushing around. The doctor smeared it on the floor as she moved. And it still grew, dripping in a steady flow from the gurney Annalise was lying on.

Screaming sounded in my ears, a howl that couldn't have been human.

Why aren't they stopping it?

"Get him out," the doctor shouted now, not pausing what she was doing.

The anesthetist injected Annalise with something, calling out numbers and playing around with the machinery. His next utterance stopped my heart, shattering it into a million pieces.

"Resus."

That word. That one word. *Resus.*

She was going to die.

She couldn't die.

No! "Don't you die, Anna. Don't you fucking

die," I shouted, my voice hoarse. Another set of arms closed around me, tugging me back. I couldn't hold on, couldn't stop them pulling me out. "Don't you let her die." My desperate cries ripped through the air, falling on deaf ears as the doors whooshed shut in front of me. I fought, kicking and screaming to get back to her, but it was no use.

I found myself in a room. It was quiet, serene—the exact opposite of the turmoil raging through me. I needed my sister to be okay. I couldn't lose her. Her baby needed her.

The baby.

My mind blanked and the room spun. The man's strong arms hadn't left me, but they'd loosened when the fight left my body. I was led over to the plastic chairs and helped into one. My limbs were heavy, my heart in pieces.

Tears tracked down my face unchecked, one landing on my hand. The wetness drew my eyes, and I looked at the splatter on my skin and against my darker hairs.

The aide's deep voice broke the silence. "Is there someone we can call?" He was crouching in front of me, peering at me with a concerned expression.

"Dad. He's in the waiting room." My response was quiet, broken like I was. We couldn't lose her.

He nodded and stood, turning to walk out of the room.

"Wait," I called. "The baby. What's she had? Where is he?"

"She had a girl. A very healthy, perfect little girl. She's being cared for in the nursery until you're ready to see her."

"A girl," I murmured. "She wants a girl." When he opened the door, my breath caught and I choked out, "Please save her." I was begging, but I wasn't ashamed of that. I'd do anything to save her, sell my soul to the Devil himself if it meant Annalise would live. She was meant for great things. She was meant to save people, to protect them, to turn into an old woman watching her little girl grow up, not to die before she'd even met her baby. Not her. Not someone who had so much to give and had so much to live for.

"The doctors in there are the best at what they do. Your sister is in good hands." He gave me a small nod that was probably supposed to be reassuring and walked out, quietly shutting the door behind him. It wasn't lost on me that he hadn't promised a thing.

It was like I was having an out-of-body experience, watching myself sit and stare at the wall. Hours had to have passed before my father rushed in, looking wild-eyed and panicked. The room erupted with activity when he pushed through the door, demanding to know what was going on. The aide pointed to the chair next to me, but Dad refused to sit, snapping at him to answer his questions. Pacing in front of me, he was all anxious energy and flying hands as the aide tried to explain that there were complications and the doctor would be out to talk to us once she had an update.

I couldn't move. My body was numb. The walls were closing in on me, and I couldn't breathe. I was cold down to my bones, frozen like ice had been poured through my veins. Trapped in a nightmare that was all too real. I was waiting to wake up, for Ashton Kutcher to stick his head in and yell, "Punk'd." For anything except the reality that had my world crashing down around me.

Why? Why her? Why now?

Sick to my stomach, my vision spotted, blacking out on the edges, and I swayed in my seat.

The aide was beside me in an instant. "Breathe, buddy. Come on, take a breath for me." He rubbed my back and I took a gasping breath, my lungs burning. "That's it. Take another one." I did that too and he pulled back, giving me some space. "I'm going to check on your sister and the baby. Does Annalise have a name picked out yet?"

"Grace, after our nan. She wants to call her Gracie."

"That's a beautiful name." He patted me on the back. "I'll go check on Gracie, okay?"

We waited for what could've been an eternity. Dad paced. I sat with my fingers interlinked, elbows resting on my bouncing knees. Each second passed by slower than the one before, the ticking of my watch thundering in my ears.

When the door pushed open, I jumped up, but the look on the doctor's face said it all. The air rushed out of my lungs and my legs gave way beneath me. My knees hit the cold linoleum, the sharp pain a welcome distraction. I fisted my hands by my sides, but they still shook.

She was gone. The realization slammed into me like a freight train at full speed, shattering my body and my soul.

Wailing filled my ears, the screams of "no" filled with utter agony. It was me making the noise, me crying and sobbing, begging for the doctor to be wrong. Begging for this nightmare to end and my sister to walk through the door.

She was so alive, so beautiful and perfect. She was supposed to be the best mom out there. Why did this happen to her? Why? It was so fucking unfair.

She didn't deserve it. None of us did, especially not Grace.

"Oh God, Gracie."

"She can't be gone. She can't be gone." Dad was repeating himself over and over, rocking in his seat.

My baby sister was dead. She was gone. My heart was crushed, lying shattered in a million shards of splintered glass. I ached. I wanted to reach out and hold her, to bicker with her and tease her. But I'd never get the chance again. And her baby girl would never know her. She'd miss out on all the wonderful things about Annalise.

I curled in on myself, hugging my legs and rocking on the floor. All I could see was bleakness stretched out before me, a world without color. Not even the light was as bright. It was as if Anna had sucked all that was good out of the world when she was torn from it.

Shuffling and footsteps behind me made me glance up, and I saw Dad stand. He looked as broken as I was, as beaten down and trodden on by life. Fate, if that's what this was, was a cruel bitch, one I'd love to kick the shit out of if I ever came face-to-face with her.

"Dad," I whimpered, not wanting to be left alone.

"He's going to the chapel, Mr. Lambert. Would you like to go with him before we talk?"

"What?" I asked, confused. "No. No, I... where's Anna?" I got to my feet, my bones creaking like I'd aged decades in thirty minutes, and walked to the door. I needed to see her, but the doctor's gentle words had me pausing.

"You can see her in a minute. We're looking after Annalise for you."

I rested my forehead against the cold steel of the doorframe, my hand on the knob. "What happened? What went wrong?"

"Annalise had what's called a uterine atony. It basically means that her uterus failed to contract after we got Grace out. It caused a severe hemorrhage."

"Did it hurt her?" I turned and looked at the doctor, sitting in the chair across the room. She'd changed her scrubs and no longer wore the gloves and face mask. Sadness hovered around her too.

"No, Caden. She didn't feel it." She took a breath and wiped away a tear. "Annalise was an amazing person. She'd become a good friend since she was stationed here. I'm so sorry that she's not here to care for her baby."

"I don't know what to do," I whispered, tears springing to my eyes again. "I don't know how to look after Gracie. I don't even know if I can. What happens if her father wants her? I don't know who he is."

"Do you want to look after Grace? Will you raise her?" Her tone held no judgment, but it was like a kick to the chest. I'd wanted to be in that baby's life from the day I found out about her. I'd never abandon her, never even dream of letting another soul take her. If Anna wasn't here, her baby was mine to love and cherish and raise. I loved her and I hadn't even met her. I'd fight for her until the day I died. Just like I would've happily handed my soul over to save my sister, I'd do the same for her baby.

"Yes," I choked out. "I'll do whatever it takes. I just need to know what *it* is."

"And your sister didn't tell you who the baby's father is?" I shook my head. "All I can say is that Annalise told me he'd signed over parental rights to her a few months ago. The lawyer on base looked after it for her. He'll be able to help you."

"What about Anna?" I paused. I couldn't get the words out. Just thinking about burying my sister crushed me again. "And Gracie?"

"You aren't alone. There are a lot of support services for families. I'll put some people in touch with you to prepare the funeral and help care for Grace."

"Can I see them now?"

The doctor nodded and walked me out. I followed her, numb, unfeeling. Or maybe it was the opposite—maybe I was drowning in pain. I didn't know. It was hard to breathe, as if my lungs were being crushed.

I found myself standing before a door, but I had to work up the courage to push through it. Knowing Anna was on the other side of it had me swallowing past the lump in my throat, but I had to do it. I needed to tell her that I'd take care of Gracie, love her like she would have.

It took a good minute of me steeling myself to be able to push through and walk into the small room. What I saw took my breath away, the air rushing out of my lungs as my knees began to fold under me.

Anna, my baby sister, so full of life and bright and happy, so strong and feisty, lay unmoving on the table. So ashen. So still. Her vivid green eyes would be forever unseeing behind her closed lids, her long eyelashes fanning out on her pale cheeks. Her lips, normally turned up in a smile, were blue.

Walking across that room took me an age. The simple act of putting one foot in front of the other took every ounce of strength I possessed. My lungs seized as I stepped up to her, the little girl I'd watched grow up to be a woman I admired and adored lying there. Dead. Forever gone. I reached out to her, my hand shaking so badly that I had to pause for a breath to center myself. I touched her hand, curling my fingers around hers, and I couldn't have stopped the sob that escaped my lips even if I'd tried. Heaving cries erupted from me, the reality of losing her hitting me all over again.

She wasn't squeezing my hand. She wasn't moving. She wasn't shushing my cries or pinching my nipple, trying to get a rise out of me. There were no snarky comments. There was just nothing.

"Anna," I cried. "We need you. I don't know how to do this. I'm not strong like you. Why can't you come back? Why'd you have to leave?" I dashed the tears away with the heel of my free hand, then rested my forehead on our joined hands. "You had a baby girl. I haven't met her yet, but I will soon. I can't wait, but God, I wish you were here. I'd do anything, fucking anything, to have you back." My tears were falling hard, my voice choked up. And yet she still didn't move. She never would again.

In that moment, a piece of me broke, never to be whole again. Life wasn't supposed to happen like this. It wasn't supposed to punish an innocent baby. It wasn't supposed to punish my beautiful sister.

"I'll look after Gracie for you, Anna. Raise her right, just like you would've wanted. I'll be a better man for her. I'll protect her. I'll never let anything bad happen to her. I promise."

Time was passing too fast and yet too slow at the

same time. I knew in my heart that every second with Annalise was one I couldn't get back with Grace, and she needed me now more than anyone. Gracie was my life now, which meant I needed to say goodbye.

Through the tears falling, I looked upon my sister one last time. My beloved, beautiful baby sister. I ran my fingers through her hair and took in a shuddering breath. "I love you, Anna, but I need to go now. Watch over us, yeah? Guide me. Hell, I dunno, give me something to let me know I'm not completely fucking things up." I kissed her forehead and squeezed my eyes closed, willing the tears to stop for just one second. "Bye, Anna."

If I thought walking in was hard, walking away broke me. With every step, my soul was wrenched out and stomped on. I was ravaged by the storm by the time I reached the door, and going through it crushed me. The doctor was waiting outside the room for me but gave me space. I leaned back against the wall and breathed deep, trying to pull myself together again. I was coming apart at the seams, unraveling, but I was desperate to hold it together.

My voice sounded hollow, just as broken as me. "Dad wasn't coping. He… there's something wrong with him. He hasn't been the same since Mom died. Now Anna. I dunno if he's gonna be strong enough."

"I can put him in touch with someone to talk to.

There are techniques that help. You should go too, Caden. Counseling will help you process everything."

I nodded. At that point, I'd take whatever help I could get.

"Can I meet Gracie now? I need to explain. I know it sounds stupid, but Anna would want that. She'd want Gracie to know how much her mom loved her."

I sucked in a breath, trying to stop myself from crying, but I couldn't. I was trying to be happy, to be excited that I would meet my little niece soon, but everything was raw, utterly overwhelming. It was like a hurricane had ripped through me, swallowing me up and spitting me out, leaving me mangled and broken in its wake.

"It doesn't sound stupid, Caden. Not at all." The doctor moved over to me, resting a hand on my arm. "Come with me to the nursery."

CHAPTER 4
CADEN

The landscape of the hallways changed as we walked, going from clinical to brightly dressed with happy colors and artwork along the walls. Laughter echoed from rooms, and I received smiles from every person I passed. It should've been us. We should've been happy, Anna lying in bed cuddling Gracie with a smile on her face a mile wide. Instead, my insides were shredded, a bloodied mess.

The doctor stopped in front of a glass wall looking into a small room with murals of rolling fields and farm animals, bright sunshine and fluffy clouds adorning the walls. It was dimly lit, and a nurse walked between the four miniature cots on wheels, checking on the swaddled babies. Each one had a surname at the foot of the cot. I held my breath when I took a step closer, pausing at the glass.

Another man was there, watching his baby. The doctor spoke in a hushed tone. "I'll go get her so you can meet her."

The other man turned to me and saw the tears rolling down my cheeks. "Missed the birth or overwhelmed? It's a pretty big moment."

I shook my head but didn't answer him. I couldn't. I didn't want to bare my soul to this stranger.

"Which baby is yours?" he prodded, ignoring my discomfort.

"Gracie," I whispered. "Grace Lambert." I pointed to the cot where the doctor was now standing and heard a choked gasp come from the man next to me.

"Oh, um… yeah," he mumbled, taking a step back. I was instantly on edge, but I had no idea why.

"Who were you watching?" I asked, trying to figure out what it was about him that had alarm bells ringing.

"Um." He hesitated and his shoulders dropped. "You're Caden, aren't you?" It wasn't a question. He knew me, but I had no idea who he was. "Annalise spoke of you often. I'm the baby's father. Anna messaged me yesterday to tell me that she was coming in. I felt like I had to visit, you know?"

"No, I don't." I bristled. "Why now? When

you've given up your rights? Don't think you're gonna change your mind."

"I'm not. I just... I suppose I wanted to come by and wish Anna well." He pointed to the nurse's station that I'd walked past but hadn't noticed and continued, "The nurses wouldn't tell me where she is. Figured she's in recovery or something, so I thought I'd check out what the baby looked like."

I didn't even know what to feel. My gut told me to beat the shit out of him, to make him hurt as much as I was, but then the doctor walked out, Gracie in her arms. I turned to the tiny baby, but he snagged my attention again, tapping me on the arm with an envelope. "Here, maybe you could give her this. My wife always likes it when I buy her this stuff."

The doctor stepped back, putting some space between Grace and me when I stiffened. "Your wife?" I spat out. "You cheated on your wife with Annalise?"

"No." He shook his head. "We were taking a break. Anna's fun and hot, but we just hooked up. It didn't mean anything." He winced when he saw the thunderous look on my face, but the idiot just kept on talking. "My wife had already asked me to come home when I found out Anna was knocked up. I couldn't have another kid. It would've ended my marriage."

It took everything in me not to beat the bastard to a pulp. I knew my emotions were running close to the surface—I didn't have the energy to filter them—but like an idiot, the dude kept his back ramrod straight and his hand extended.

I took the embossed envelope made of heavy cardstock and, out of morbid curiosity, asked through gritted teeth, "What's in it?"

"Voucher for some lingerie."

I clenched my jaw shut so tight I was sure I'd crack a molar. This guy was a piece of work. He was giving his baby mama a lingerie voucher hours after she'd given birth to a baby he wanted nothing to do with. Talk about disrespecting her. He was a piece of shit, completely unworthy of my sister. Thinking about him taking advantage of her, using her as a way to blow off steam when he was single and could fuck around, made me want to kill him. But my niece didn't deserve that. I wouldn't let the first thing she saw be me getting hauled off in cuffs for beating the ever-loving shit out of her sperm donor.

I stepped up to him until we were chest to chest. He was a few inches taller than me—I barely came up to his chin—but I was pissed enough that he flinched when I growled, "I don't want to see you near her ever again. Not here, not at the house. Never. Again. You hear me?"

"You can't keep me from Anna. If I want to see her, I'll damn well see her."

"Only if I fucking kill you, you bastard."

"That's enough, gentlemen," a guy in military uniform interrupted. "Sir, if you'll step this way." He faced the dick I was talking to and pointed down the corridor.

They began walking and I turned away. It was on the tip of my tongue to tell him what happened, but something held me back. What if he tried to take Gracie from me? I couldn't risk it.

When I turned to the baby girl in the doctor's arms, the rest of the world fell away and mine tilted on its axis. She was perfect. A tiny bundle of perfection. I'd never seen a creature as beautiful or precious as her. Her lips were pouty, her button nose pink-tipped. Her long dark eyelashes, just like her mother's, fanned over her cheeks as she slept. Her dusting of hair was the same dark brown as my sister's too. Her tiny hands were curled into tight little fists near her chin, the only parts of her I could see with the sheet tightly wrapped around her.

The doctor held her out to me and I took her gratefully, cradling her head and snuggling her against my body. I took a slow breath in and began crying for a totally different reason. Pure and unfettered joy filled me. Love like I'd never experienced before pulsed through me. In that moment, I gave my heart and soul to her. This baby girl, my niece and now my daughter-to-be, had from that second onward become my life.

"Hi, baby girl. Your name is Gracie. Your mama named you after our nan. Welcome to the world, sweetheart." Her eyelids fluttered, and I cupped her tiny head, running my thumb over her forehead. "I love you, Gracie. More than anything on this earth. Your mama did too. She didn't want to leave, but she didn't have a choice." I brushed the tears off my cheeks with my shoulder, trying not to disturb Grace too much. "God, I miss her so much already, but you remind me of her. You're gonna be beautiful and strong and smart just like her."

Gracie blinked open her eyes and yawned before letting out a tiny cry that was more like the bleat of a lamb than the wail of a baby. My breath caught as I looked in her eyes, and I let out a sob. "I'm such a mess, but I promise I'll get better. I'll be the best I can for you. Whatever it takes, I promise you. But you gotta help me, yeah? We're a team. It's us against the world." I reached for her balled-up fist, and she curled her fingers around my pinkie, squeezing tight.

Her cries intensified, and I figured I needed to do something, although I had no idea what.

The doctor, who'd been standing off to one side

checking paperwork, rested a hand on my arm. "Would you like the nurses to show you how to change and feed her?"

"Yes, please." I nodded, unable to look away from my baby girl. "Do you think the lawyer will be able to help me adopt her?"

"He will." The warmth in her voice had me looking up. "You'll make a great dad, Caden. Gracie's lucky to have you."

I spent the next half hour going through changing and feeding and burping Gracie before Dad stuck his head in the room.

"Dad," I greeted him, unable to help the excitement in my voice. "She's so beautiful. You have to see her." I smiled at him and stood up, Gracie in my arms.

"I can't," he murmured quietly. "I... I have to go."

I halted my steps and took a moment to think over what he'd just said. Confusion filled me. "What? What do you mean you have to go?" Where the hell was more important than right there? Anna and Gracie were our only priorities.

"I need to get out of here, Caden. I can't breathe. I can't stay."

"Dad, we need to stick together. I need you. Gracie needs you. I can't do this alone. We both need to grieve, I get it, but please don't leave me alone," I begged, gently placing Gracie in her cot.

"No." He shook his head, backing out toward the door. "I have to go."

"No you don't." I was being harsh with him, but I couldn't let him check out on me. I caught his arm as he stepped out of the room and held him there. "I know what you're going through. Remember, I just lost my sister too, and Mom a few months ago. I know they were the loves of your life. They were mine too. But that baby in there? She needs us to be strong for her. We're everything to her now, and she deserves the best of us."

He looked at me sadly and shook my arm off. "I'll see you tonight when you get home, Caden. I can't stay."

"I won't be coming home until Gracie's ready to come with me. Please don't do anything stupid, Dad." My emotions were riding the surface again, my voice hitching. "I can't bury you too."

"I won't. I just need to be out on the water for a while." He stepped back and the desolation in his eyes was palpable. "You'll be a good father."

"Don't you dare speak to me like you're not coming back, Dad." I lurched forward and grabbed his shirt, hauling him to me. He was frail in my arms, like he'd turned into an old man in the blink of an eye. It was no wonder why. "I love you."

He held me tight, squeezing just as hard as I was hugging him. His tears fell then, soaking my shirt while I somehow managed to hold it together. All I could think about was Gracie. How much she needed me, how she deserved a wonderful life. My sister should've been there to give it to her, but I was privileged to stand in her place.

"I love you too, son."

MASON

July

THERE WAS NO ANSWER TO MY CALLS. FOR THREE WEEKS I'd been trying to reach Caden, but he didn't pick up. There were no return messages, nothing. I didn't have much experience with newborns, so I might've been totally off base, but surely he'd have a free moment when his sister was feeding the baby or when it was sleeping. Hell, I was still calling the baby an "it." I didn't even know whether Annalise had had a girl or boy.

"Still no answer?" Ricky asked me as I palmed my cell, my shoulders slumping after I ended the call. His message bank was probably full—I'd loaded it up, begging him to call me, or anyone if he decided he didn't want to talk. I was worried. It was unlike him to go for so long without answering. Even when we weren't speaking, he responded to my messages quicker than he was doing now.

"No." I shook my head. "Shouldn't he have called? He said we had a lot to talk about. I didn't think he was gonna cut me off." I hated the neediness in my voice, but I was too old to deny how much I wanted him in my life. I wanted more than friendship too. I had no idea if anything would ever come of my attraction, but even if it didn't, I couldn't lose that. He meant too much to me for me to just let him go.

Ricky surprised me, stepping closer until he could reach up and cup my face. I tried not to act surprised, basking in the warmth of the other man's palm against my skin. I didn't want him to let go; I wanted him just as much as Caden. I didn't even think it was possible. Being attracted to two people at a time was the kind of stuff that only happened in porn, but there was something there. A spark. Want. Need.

Ricky had been showing me more of himself of late, letting me know that he enjoyed both men and women. He treated me differently to his friends, touching me on my hip or placing his big hand at the small of my back when we were together. He didn't do the back-slapping hug and double-cheeked kiss he gave to Reef and Ford with me either. Instead, he held me a little longer, a little tighter, before letting me go and giving me the odd smile that looked almost shy.

His touches, though few and far between, had bolstered my confidence, but it also had my mind running wild with fantasies I was almost desperate to act out. The idea that he could pin me against whatever surface he wanted and get me to submit—even though I knew he'd never take what wasn't freely given—was such a turn-on that it had my dick leaking whenever I thought about it. Add in thoughts of what Caden would be doing with us, and I usually shot my load so damn fast it was embarrassing.

But it wasn't just the possibility of sex with them—I wanted so much more. I had these daydreams of us in ten years toasting marshmallows on the fire in the iron pit Ricky had on his back deck, and it was heaven. The idea that I could find that kind of happiness had been a pipe dream for so many years I couldn't count. I could've quit traveling around and settled down anytime, but I hadn't found anyone I wanted to have that sort of future with. And now I couldn't think of anything else, anyone else I wanted.

I wasn't sure why I was comfortable with the idea of being attracted to men. In my forty-one years on this planet, I hadn't even looked at a man that way before, never mind two, but I couldn't deny that my attraction to both Ricky and Caden existed. I didn't want to deny it. I hadn't quite figured out whether I was sexually fluid and the change was normal, albeit a late one for me, or I'd discovered I was actually bisexual, pansexual, in denial, or just completely blind for most of my life up to that point. Whichever way I labeled myself, it honestly didn't worry me so much. It was kind of a revelation, actually, like I'd been in the shadows all that time and I'd just walked out into bright sunlight.

Except now I was wondering where that revelation would leave me if Caden wouldn't even return my calls. I had no idea how to move things forward with either of them. Even though Ricky was becoming more affectionate, he'd back off after every touch. It was one step forward and two steps back with us. I feared it was going to be even worse with Caden. He'd let slip one night in the quiet of the hotel room we were sharing that he was gay. I don't know if he remembered it afterward—he was so sleep-deprived that he was almost delirious. It was only when I pulled him into my arms that he relaxed enough to catch a few Z's. Since then, since holding him and having him go lax in my arms, his body vulnerable in sleep, I'd wanted more. Now I didn't even know where I stood.

That uncertainty was my fault though. I'd reported him to the World Anti-Doping Agency. I'd been the one to start the ball rolling that ended his career. Or perhaps more accurately, the career after his time on the snowboarding pro circuit ended. He'd planned on retiring anyway, but he had media gigs lined up and sponsorships that would've continued for years afterward. Then he tested positive for THC, and that was the end of that.

He found out in the worst way possible too—overhearing me telling our friends. I'd planned on talking to him, but I was scared to death of losing him. That fear had stopped me from being honest with him. It was selfish, absolutely a dick move on my part.

My reasons for speaking with Reef and Ford about it were completely innocent. I was only trying to figure out how to tell Caden without completely destroying whatever we had. I'd already ruined enough things for him, so I was just trying to soften the news that I'd been responsible for it all. Even though I hadn't had a choice, and I certainly didn't want to report it, I'd had to. My accreditation as a coach came with the condition that I blow the whistle on any suspected drug use. I'd held off as long as I could, trying to give him the benefit of the doubt, but there was no way I could let it go when I walked into his hotel room and the cloying smell of weed hit me like a ton of bricks. His clothes reeked of it, but that wasn't proof in and of itself. I hadn't wanted to believe it, but Caden's eyes left me with no doubt that he was stoned.

Even still, I hadn't wanted to believe it was intentional, but I couldn't not do anything either. I knew it'd affect his career, but the legitimacy we'd worked so hard to establish in the competition would be shot if I covered it up, even through omission. It'd do irreversible damage. Reporting him was the right thing to do to keep the sport professional, and there was no doubt that competitors like Reef and Caden were professionals. Drugs weren't tolerated in running or swimming or any of the team sports, so it couldn't be acceptable in snowboarding either. Still, making the call was the hardest thing I'd ever done.

Now I had to live with the consequences. Had I irreparably damaged our friendship? Had I managed to squash any potential that we'd become more? I didn't know, but the silence was speaking volumes at that point.

What I did know was that we were dancing around each other. Tiptoeing awkwardly because none of us knew the rules. All I wanted to do was dive in headfirst, but I knew I couldn't. Where did I even start? I wanted Caden, but I didn't know whether he was prepared to even speak to me anymore. If he wasn't, what would that mean for Ricky? I didn't want to put him in a position where he'd have to choose between his friend or his lover, and getting involved with either one of them would mean exactly that.

I had to speak to Caden, had to check on him.

I wanted to hear his voice too. Needed it.

I blew out a frustrated breath and Ricky wrapped his arm around me, finally giving me the contact I so desperately needed. I turned in his arms and hugged him tightly, breathing him in. The play of his muscles under my hands made me moan softly, and I felt rather than heard the hitch of his breath. I may have been stupidly pushing for something I had no business wanting, but I couldn't help it. I brushed my lips over his temple and nuzzled against him.

Ricky's reaction was instantaneous. His fingers pressed into my back, gripping me harder as he blew out a harsh breath. Pulling back, I looked into his eyes before dropping my gaze to his lips. Those lips were made for kissing, and damn did I want to feast on them. I was drawn to him like a planet orbiting the sun, and I leaned in closer.

He wasn't having it. Dropping his arms, Ricky stepped back and turned away from me, snatching his cell from the countertop. "Let me try calling him."

I blew out a breath and fought the stab of pain in my chest. It was probably for the best; attraction was one thing, but him getting in the middle of the mess I'd created was quite another.

I scrubbed my hand across my forehead and nodded.

"Yeah, please."

He held the cell up to his ear and waited, drumming his fingers against the countertop he'd moved near. A shake of his head told me all I needed to know—Caden hadn't picked up. "Caden, we're worried about you. Call us or text, whatever. We just want to know that everything's okay."

He hung up and gently put his cell down on the bench. Ricky looked like he wanted to say something, but I couldn't hear it. I also couldn't sit around waiting for a call that probably wouldn't come. The walls were closing in on me. I needed to get out of there, to do something.

I spun on my heels and strode upstairs, changing into workout clothes. I was going for a run.

RICCARDO

The door slammed shut as Mason left, and I wanted to kick myself.

God. Fuck. Damn it. Why didn't I let him kiss me?

I'd been hesitant at first because he was so skittish. I wasn't convinced that Mason even really knew what he wanted, what he was getting himself into. I'd wait as long as he needed, but when he gave himself to me, I'd want all of him. Until he was sure he could give it, I wouldn't take the chance. Couldn't. He'd already captured a piece of me, and I didn't want to lose more of myself to him.

But that was the thing—it wasn't only Mason I craved. I wanted Caden just as much, and I couldn't imagine one without the other. But did Mason want the same? Sure, they were friends, and it was obvious how desperate Mason was to get Caden to start speaking to him again after his monumental fuckup, but that didn't necessarily translate into being ready to—or even wanting to—jump into a triad relationship. I wished Mason had been upfront with him about the drug test. Caden would've eventually seen that Mason really had no choice. He would've forgiven him. What he might not forgive was Mason's lie—by omission, but a lie nevertheless.

So there I was, confused as fuck. *What the hell should I do?* The idea of craving two people wasn't the problem. I'd grown up in a pretty progressive household, especially for uber-Catholic Italy. My parents had an open relationship and never hid it from us, so I understood polyamory, having lived it for most of my childhood. The relationship wasn't the issue either—I'd seen three people in a relationship work more than once. My problem was with others' perceptions. Or maybe it was just what I thought of myself.

I was pansexual. I'd spent the better part of half my life explaining my sexuality to people, and they still didn't get it. They always assumed it was a phase, that I'd eventually be able to make up my mind. Or they'd say if I wasn't entirely straight, I was really a closeted gay man, because God forbid that attraction was fluid and could change. They had no idea; attraction to them was black and white. I'd fought hard to dispel the ignorant assumptions that I was really gay, or that I was into wild orgies because I could be attracted to all genders.

Finding myself wanting both Caden and Mason challenged everything I thought I stood for. I suddenly wanted wild orgies with them. But I'd been hemming and hawing, flip-flopping from hot to cold for weeks. I'd convinced myself that I was waiting for Mason to give me some sign that he wanted the same things as me. Maybe I was holding things up while I tried to come to terms with the fact that I was more like my parents than I cared to admit.

Mason was being patient with me, but I could tell it was wearing thin. He was confused, couldn't understand why I'd touch him or react to him, then pull away. Every time I did it, I regretted it more. I was thirty-eight years old, old enough to know better than to hurt either one of them, but I had to be certain. I couldn't risk losing either of them, and I knew choosing one over the other would end it for all of us.

The cell phone beside me sang out, though it wasn't my ringtone but Mason's. Caden's name flashed on the screen, and I didn't hesitate to answer it. Mason would be livid if I didn't, and hell, I was just as worried about Caden as he was.

"Caden, hey. It's Rick." My relief was obvious in my tone.

There was a pause before he whispered, "Rick." His voice was rough, and the despair behind it broke me. Raw pain, complete and absolute. I tried to suck in a breath, but my chest had constricted like a vise.

"What's going on?" I gripped the edge of the

countertop, terrified of what his answer would be. Something was very, very wrong. Even hearing just that one word, I knew it was so much worse than when he'd been suspended from competition.

"It's all gone to shit." His breath hitched, and I heard him taking a few deep breaths. "I'm in so fucking far over my head."

I had no idea what to say, no clue how to make it right. But I needed to. "Baby not letting you sleep?" I hedged, trying to get more out of him.

"Not really. She's crying nonstop. She wants to feed constantly, but when I give her the bottle, she suckles but doesn't really drink. I can't put her down. I can't sleep, can't eat. I haven't had a shower in days because she screams when she's in her cot, and I'm too scared I'll drop her if I take her in with me. I can't do anything without her in my arms. I've managed to get her to sleep in her swing, but it's only ever for a few minutes. It's the first time in three days that she's slept anywhere but on my chest."

He was worried, exhausted and frustrated. It was obvious that he was stressed and so frazzled that he was beside himself. But why was she sleeping on his chest? Why wouldn't his sister stay with her at least part of the time?

"How's Annalise?" There was no answer for a long time, but I could hear him crying through the phone. "Caden, talk to me," I pleaded, my heart breaking at his pain.

"She's dead," he rasped, the utter grief in those two words ripping me apart. *Oh God.* "She bled out during the C-section. Docs couldn't save her." He blew out a breath and his voice steadied a bit. "The autopsy showed no one was at fault."

"Fuck. I'm so sorry. I can't imagine how hard it's been for you and your pops to go through that." My voice cracked when I spoke. My mind was spinning, reeling from the news, and my heart hurt. Caden and his father had suffered so much, lost so much, and now they were looking after a baby while grieving a loss that would've cut them soul deep.

"Dad's not here."

The silence lingered between us when I repeated his words in my head. "What do you mean? Where is he?"

"On the boat. He left just after it happened. He comes back for maybe an hour at a time, but he won't come inside, won't stay. He says he can't, that it reminds him too much of Annalise. Even after the funeral when everyone was here, he wouldn't come in. Sat in the damn chair in the garden staring out into space."

Shock, grief, and anger coursed through me. I wanted to shake his father until I knocked some sense into him, but in some way, I understood that the loss of the two women he loved more than any others in the world had broken him. Caden had confided in us that his mother's death had changed the man he looked up to. I knew his father would be unrecognizable now. I couldn't hate him for that, but leaving Caden alone to grieve and cope with no support wasn't right. That's not what family did. They pulled together. They dropped everything and pitched in for as long as it was needed.

"We're gonna help, okay? We're gonna get you whatever you need, do whatever it takes. You're not alone in this, Caden."

"You don't need—"

"Yes, I do, because that's what people do for their friends, their family. We chip in and help. I can't let you struggle when I can do something. Don't ask me to do that."

Caden's response was quiet but strong. "Thank you." I heard crying in the background, and the noise made something in my heart flip and a smile break out.

Caden had a baby. He was a dad.

"What's her name?"

I could hear the smile in his voice when he spoke. "Gracie, after our grandmother."

"That's beautiful." I paused, smiling. "Can you send us a photo? We'd love to see her."

"Yeah, I can. Filled up my cell's memory already. Her eyes are starting to turn green like Anna's." He sniffed and a rustling sounded through the line as the crying became louder.

"I'll speak to you soon, okay? Keep your cell near you. I'll text before we call to make sure it's a good time for you."

"I will." He paused momentarily before continuing. "Rick? Thanks again."

"Anytime."

I hung up, letting him get back to Gracie, and closed my eyes, tears dripping down my cheeks. I couldn't imagine what he was going through. All I knew was that I needed to help, needed to take some of his heartache away.

I typed out a quick message to Reef and Ford, asking them to come over urgently. Ford was a paramedic; surely he'd be able to help, give Caden some advice. Even if it was just moral support, I knew they'd do what they could.

MASON

After my hour-long run, I stumbled back in to find Ricky joined by Reef and Ford in the living room, two of them on computers and Reef on the phone pacing. There was a hive of activity, but the air hung heavy in the room. It was tense, unusual for the three men. More often than not when we were together, there were jokes and teasing all around.

Sweaty and desperate for a drink, I held up my hand, stopping Ricky from saying whatever it was he had to say, and headed straight for the kitchen. Pouring myself a glass of water straight from the faucet, I chugged it down before repeating the action and swallowing another half a glass. I wiped my balled-up T-shirt across my face and down my chest before I turned back to him.

Ricky walked over to me. Something had happened in the time I'd been gone. He'd been crying, that much I could tell, and he was barely holding it together now. I tossed my sweaty shirt aside and reached out for him, grasping his biceps and gently squeezing them. "What's wrong?"

"Caden called you while you were gone." Ricky shook his head and took a deep breath, blinking rapidly.

"What's going on? You're scaring me." There was

a wobble in my voice that I didn't even try to disguise.

"Caden's sister died during the C-section."

Ricky continued speaking after that, but white noise had filled my ears, a buzzing so loud that I could see his lips moving but couldn't hear a single thing he said. Shock rocked me to my core. I dropped my hands and stumbled back, leaning against the wall for support. I was shaking my head, pleading, begging that the words weren't true. He'd already lost so much; he couldn't lose his sister too. He adored her. She was his best friend, his inspiration, and his rock.

"Mason, focus." Ricky had his warm hands on my cheeks, his strong body so close I could feel the heat radiating from him. "We're helping him, okay? We're trying to get to him."

"What about the baby?" I questioned, my heart racing.

"Annalise had a baby girl and she's fine, but Caden's not coping." He fished his cell out of his pocket and showed me a photo of the sweetest baby with blue-green eyes staring at the camera, bottle in her mouth. "He named her Gracie."

A little girl. I couldn't help the small smile that tilted my lips when I thought about him raising a beautiful daughter, but it quickly slipped when I pictured him doing it alone.

"That's not all, Mason. His dad's pretty much checked out." Ricky shook his head sadly. "He's barely there, and when he is, he stares out to space. He's not helping. He's not even with it. Caden's on his own."

"We need to bring him home, Ricky," I breathed, stepping closer to him. I needed him, needed to have him in my arms, to comfort him. I wanted Caden there too, wished I could have him between us to care for and treasure.

Ricky wrapped his arms around me as I did the same to him, and we sank into each other's embrace, clinging to one another for support. I closed my eyes and turned my face into his neck, breathing in his spicy scent. I couldn't help brushing my lips over his collarbone. When he shivered, I did it again, trailing soft kisses up the column of his throat, along his jaw to the side of his mouth.

"Whatcha doin', Mason?" Ricky moaned softly.

"Kissing you." It wasn't a question. I wasn't asking for permission. I was taking, and finally giving. As much as I wanted to slam my lips against his, to ravage him, leaving him with kiss-swollen lips and panting for breath, I couldn't. Everything in me screamed to show him that it wasn't just about sex for me. He meant so much more than that.

I brushed my lips against his in a gentle press, once and then twice before drawing away. I was intoxicated by the touch of his lips against mine, firm but soft all at the same time, rough and smooth too. As far as first kisses went, it was a hell of a lot more innocent than any of my first kisses with girls, but it was so right. So perfect. It wasn't just about hot desire and hard, sweaty sex. It was a promise, but something else too.

I really wanted more. I wanted everything, but it wasn't the time. Not only did Caden need us, but I needed a shower.

I pulled back just far enough that I could rest my forehead against his, nuzzling his nose with my own. "Do you want this, Ricky? Us?" I asked, closing my eyes. I didn't think I could bear it if he refused me.

He blew out a breath and squeezed my hips. "I do, but I'm confused."

"What about?" I opened my eyes and looked into his whiskey ones. Cupping his cheek, I stroked his stubbled jaw with my thumb, the skin above his beard warm under my touch.

"I don't just want you. I want Caden too. I don't understand the how or why, and I'm sorry if it hurts you to hear it, but I want him too. It's like you're my perfect match together, and individually too. I don't even know what to do with that. I don't do threesomes or orgies. Yes, I'm pan, but that doesn't make me a deviant." Ricky closed his eyes and shook his head, his anger and frustration with himself pouring off him in waves.

So that's what the yo-yoing was about. His uncertainty made a whole lot more sense now. I just hoped I could give him some peace of mind knowing he wasn't alone.

"I've been researching this." I smiled at him and lifted his face to mine, brushing a kiss over his lips even as he stiffened. I didn't want to upset him, but I wanted him to know that I'd been confused too. "Pansexual people are attracted to the person, not their gender, right? So while being pansexual doesn't make you greedy or unable to decide who or what you want, and it doesn't make you a cheater, it's not outside the realm of possibility that if there's more than one person who calls to you and completes you in different ways, then you could be attracted to both of them. Is it?"

"No, it's not impossible, but now I'm everything that I've always denied pansexuality is. I'm a fucking hypocrite."

"No, you're the same man you've always been, and I really like him. I'm confused too, Ricky. I've found myself wanting not one but two men. Talk about intimidating for your first time." I laughed nervously and leaned in closer. Our words were barely more than a whisper, just loud enough that even though we weren't alone in the house, only we could hear our conversation. "I can't walk away from either of you. I don't care if we fit some mold, and I couldn't give a shit what anyone else thinks about me. But I understand that you do, and that's fine. I'm not making light of your concerns. All I'm asking is that you give us a chance to figure out what could be between us." I kissed his cheek gently and stepped away from him, backing toward the stairs. "I'm gonna take a quick shower. Gimme a few minutes, and then you can tell me what I can do to help."

Ricky smiled at me, his gaze full of something that looked a lot like affection. "Let's bring our man home, Mason."

I grinned and pushed his body against the wall, cupping his cheeks. I pressed my lips against his in a hard kiss before spinning on my heels and jogging upstairs. Butterflies fluttered around my belly, even as the guilt over being happy when Caden was devastated hit me.

We were going to help him—we had to. Even if it meant getting on a plane and going to him, I'd do it. Whatever it took.

CHAPTER 5
CADEN

"So yeah, I think from what you've told me, Gracie has reflux," Ford explained. My gut clenched as I thought of all the horrible things that could mean for the beautiful baby girl finally asleep on my chest. "It's important to treat it because she's in pain. The heartburn can get pretty bad, especially if she's not reacting well to the formula. That's why she can't sleep properly and why she's wanting to suckle all the time. She's not hungry, but the motion helps her settle."

"Okay, so what do I do?" I asked, overwhelmed with worry and helplessness. All I wanted was to take away her pain, to have her gaze at me again without her little face scrunching up and her crying out in agony.

"I've ordered some things for you on an urgent

delivery, though it might be tomorrow before it arrives."

"You didn't need to do that, Ford. I could've gone out to get it," I protested, though it was probably just my pride making me do it. Having things delivered to the house was a whole lot easier than getting Gracie in the car and over to the pharmacy, especially because I had to lug around a truckload of clothes, diapers, and wipes with me in case she spewed everywhere.

"I know I didn't, but I wanted to. It's nothing for me to order some things online, but it'll make a big difference to you having the right stuff on hand." He paused momentarily while I heard clicking in the background. "Right, the first thing I got you is some over-the-counter medicine. It's the infant version of an antacid. You should take her to the doctor to get it confirmed, but if the medicine helps, that's a good sign it's reflux." Ford went on to explain that he'd also ordered special formula to reduce her heartburn and drops to ease her wind, then told me how to use each one of them.

I thanked him, and he continued in a softer voice, "It'll get better, Caden. Easier." *I hope so.* "It will, I promise." *Did I say that out loud?* "Okay, now I'm passing you to Mace."

"Caden, hey—"

"Mace, I'm sorry. I shouldn't have held a grudge. I shouldn't have been such a prick to you. I know you were only doing what you had to. I was an idiot, and I'm sorry. Life is too damn short…."

I heard his breath hitch as I squeezed my eyes closed, fighting my emotions, but I shouldn't have bothered. His words, softly spoken but filled with a core of strength, had relief pouring through me as a sob escaped. "We're coming to you, Caden. We're gonna do this together, okay? We booked a flight for tomorrow. It was the earliest we could get."

"I… I… wait, we?"

"Me and Ricky. We'll be there in a couple of days. I'll text you the flight details, but there's no need to come pick us up. We'll get a ride to your house." I blew out a breath and scrubbed my hand over my wet eyes. "Is that okay, Caden?"

"Yeah," I rasped, my voice rough with unshed tears. "Yeah, it is. I'm overwhelmed, Mace. I never thought I'd have friends like you guys, willing to drop everything and help."

Rick came on then and reassured me that we were all in it together, that I wasn't alone anymore. All I could do was hold Gracie and cry. Relief and love flowed over me in waves, cleansing the exhaustion and grief from my soul. Their two voices drifted through, calming me and whispering support. I stayed talking to them until Gracie started wiggling and let out her bleating cry that meant she was wet and uncomfortable.

It was time for her bath anyway so, carrying her in a way that she could snuggle into me again, I went into the laundry room and started filling the tub. Life was hard without Annalise, and in this house, all of her things were a constant reminder of what I'd lost, but the gift of life she'd given to Gracie brought me more joy than I ever imagined possible. I smiled down at my baby girl as I stripped her and cradled her tiny form against me until the bath was ready. She instantly relaxed when I put her into the water, letting out a contented sigh when I started rubbing her head with one hand, supporting her neck with the other.

I had no idea if I was doing things right, and I'd screwed up more than once, but Gracie was my second chance in life just as much as I was her everything. She gave my life new meaning. I had a bigger purpose thanks to her. It didn't matter what I'd done in my past, only how I loved her now and would continue to every day for the rest of my life. I hoped that one day she'd understand that everything I did for her was because of love in its purest form.

Bundling her in a dry diaper and fresh clothes after her bath, I held Gracie while I warmed the water a little before mixing in the formula one-handed. "Here you go, baby girl. Just how you like it." She wolfed it down and I patted her back with a smile on my face. I kept going, long after I would've normally stopped, and she let out a long burp. "Well done, Gracie."

Ford was right—part of the problem had been wind. I wouldn't make that mistake again.

I strapped her in her swing and hung a toy within her reach so she could play for a while. Gracie loved her green dog already, so she barely noticed when I dashed out of the room to fix her cot. Ford suggested that I put a couple of books under one end to prop up her head so gravity could do its work.

When she'd played for long enough, I swaddled her in a wrap and laid her down, leaving only the soft glow from the small lamp in the room with her.

I was starving. I'd hardly eaten all day, only managing two cups of coffee and a banana. I needed something better to eat, so I grilled the last steak I had in the house and ate two-day-old salad with it. I barely tasted either as I shoveled it down—probably a good thing, given how wilted the leaves were. I realized how pathetic my coping skills were when I opened the fridge for a water and saw food from the wake, almost two weeks earlier. Grabbing a trash bag, I cleaned it out, tossing everything that wasn't fresh and leaving it pretty much bare. On my way back in through the laundry room, I started a load of washing and took the clean clothes with me to the sofa.

Weariness settled in as I started folding Gracie's clothes, yawns coming more and more frequently. My eyelids were growing heavier as I struggled to stay awake. If I could get this stuff done before Gracie needed another feed in a couple hours, the house wouldn't look quite so bad.

My eyes snapped open when I heard Gracie's cry. *Damn it. She hasn't slept long.* I looked down and saw folded laundry all around me. So much for resting my eyes; I'd fallen asleep, for at least a little while. I raced into her bedroom and stopped when I saw the clock on the wall. She'd slept for an hour longer than she normally would.

"Hey, baby girl," I cooed when I picked her up. Her diaper and pajamas were soaked through, so I changed them and mixed another bottle of formula for her. "Here you go. Let's get your tummy filled up," I murmured soothingly. Sitting among the folded laundry on the sofa, I fed and burped her, repeating the same moves I had earlier.

This time wasn't so successful, spew quickly covering my shoulder and running down my back. A few weeks ago, I would've been a gagging mess, but now I was more worried about the gasping cries coming from Gracie. I ripped off my shirt, wiped myself off as best as I could and changed Gracie again. Rocking her until she'd settled, I tried laying her down, but it was no use. She screamed as soon as she left my arms.

"It's okay. It's okay. Please stop crying," I begged, lifting her once more and patting her back again. She eventually settled, falling into a restless sleep against my chest.

I took the chance and buckled her into her swing before running into the bathroom just as she started to cry. I didn't have time for a shower—she'd scream bloody murder if I took longer than thirty seconds to get back to her—so a washcloth would have to do. I couldn't imagine how bad I smelled—sweaty ass crack and spew were my only cologne at the moment—but it didn't matter when I thought about Gracie. We had a rough night ahead of us.

At least I'd had a chance to eat some dinner.

THE KNOCK ON THE FRONT DOOR HAD ME ALMOST falling to my knees in supplication when I saw the delivery man. It was the medicine Ford had ordered. We'd both had a hard night, Gracie because of the severe heartburn that went with reflux and me from pure exhaustion. I just wanted her to stop crying. My arms ached and my head was pounding. I was hot and sweaty, tired and miserable. I needed a break—five minutes of quiet sounded like heaven, but she just wouldn't stop.

I was in so far over my head. How the hell was I going to do this for years? I couldn't even handle weeks at it.

I scrubbed my face, trying to wake myself up, and answered the door, signing for the package before carrying it and Gracie inside.

My salvation, I hoped, came in the form of an applicator and bottle. I needed to see the doctor on base to get a diagnosis, but Ford told me this might help in the meantime. God, I hoped so. I measured it one-handed and gave Gracie a taste. She instantly scrunched her little nose up and let out a wail, clearly hating it. I groaned and forced the rest down, hoping she drank some of it even though most ended up on her shirt.

The high-pitched cry didn't stop, and my head was about to explode with the pounding my ears were receiving. I needed a minute and a lot more caffeine. I gave Gracie some tummy time, something she usually enjoyed, and trudged into the kitchen to make myself some coffee.

Mug in hand, I stood at the kitchen sink and looked out to the faded hammock in the yard. I was jealous of the peacefulness it taunted me with, a gentle breeze rustling in the trees and plenty of shade to sleep in.

Holy crap, maybe that's it. The hammock.

I downed the rest of the scalding liquid, pulled out Gracie's stroller and popped her in it, racing outside with her. There were a hell of a lot of little seeds on the hammock, about the size of a blueberry but hard, and bird shit everywhere. The tree must have been fruiting. I looked around nervously, but the birds stayed high up in the tree. Even though they were there, and I wasn't a fan of being close to rats with wings, excitement bloomed in me at the possibility of having some time outside.

With Gracie fed, changed and baby insect repellant slathered all over her, a shade cover zipped in place over her stroller that doubled as a mosquito net, and a blessed miracle, she'd fallen asleep.

Peace. Quiet. Sleep. Finally.

I climbed onto the hammock and stretched out, casting an eye over the stroller that was only a couple of feet away from me and eying the birds warily. They were nowhere near us. Relieved, I closed my eyes and let the rocking soothe me.

Water lapped at my feet, the crystal-clear liquid cool

against my skin. Sand between my toes and the warm sun on my face was heaven. I was relaxed, the tension and grief I'd been carrying around having momentarily drifted away. Finally, hope lit my path. I was lighter. Happier. I could breathe easier.

Looking around, I saw palm trees and sand castles. People strolling along the beach and kids laughing had me smiling, but it wasn't quite right. I couldn't pinpoint it, but there was something missing. Or not so much missing as something out of place. The shoreline was familiar—it was near my sister's house—so that wasn't it.

What is it?

I watched a little girl, maybe six or seven years old, splashing in the water, her long dark hair bouncing as she jumped and ran. She was adorable and my heart lit with joy. When she turned to me, her familiar green eyes calmed me. My sister lived on in Gracie. My Gracie.

Her wide smile faltered and she ran over to me. "Daddy, what's wrong? Why are you sad? Is it because you found another gray hair?"

"What?" I asked, startled. Gray hair? What the fuck? I'm not going gray. Or maybe I am. Hell, who knows. "No, baby girl. I was just thinking of your mom. She looked just like you when she was little. It made me a little sad, but happy too."

"Look, Daddy, a crab." Grace pointed to the sand right next to my foot. A crab the size of my fist scuttled around.

I held still, not wanting to startle it, but I jumped and screeched in fright as it closed its pincer around my toe. Holy fucking shit, it's going to cut it off. I kicked out, trying to dislodge it, but it was still there, poking at me.

Loud squawking filled my ears, and I sucked in a breath.

I jarred awake and opened my eyes trying to shake off the crazy dream, but what was in front of me was a nightmare. It was like a scene straight out of Alfred Hitchcock's *The Birds*. Crows everywhere, thousands of the bastards—okay, there might have only been three—were on the hammock and Gracie's stroller, eating the seeds that had dropped from the tree. I let out a shout, which was super manly and totally not a startled squeak, and kicked my foot out harder, dislodging the evil thing from me. It stared at me with its beady black eyes and I scrambled around on the hammock trying to get away from that judgmental bastard.

The swaying of the hammock was a little crazy as I pulled my feet under me and attempted to jump from it. Holding on for dear life, I tried to throw my leg over to get some purchase on the ground, but all it served to do was pitch me forward toward the hard-packed, grassy earth. Clutching at the hammock, I tried to stop my fall, but it was no use. The ground rushed up at me and I scrunched my eyes closed, trying to catch myself with my other hand. It didn't work. Reaching out for the ground just made the hammock tilt farther, and I wobbled wildly before face-planting.

Hard.

It was my least graceful landing. Ever.

I managed to shield my face from the worst of the impact, but I was now stuck. My legs were tangled in the hammock above me, and I still held onto the faded material with a death grip. Legs up in the air, face against the ground, arm splayed out sideways, I was relieved that I was the only one home who was capable of taking photographic proof of my complete and utter inability to stay upright.

I tried to pull my legs free, but I was trapping myself with the way I held the hammock, so I let go, landing in a heap on the ground, and groaned. *Shit.* Picking my sorry ass up, I dusted myself off and gritted my teeth. *Fucking birds.*

Eying the giant steaming trail of shit down Gracie's stroller, I called out to the beady-eyed fuckers, "Really, you bastards?" At least it wasn't on her. "Couldn't just leave me to have a damn nap and not go all creepy psycho-killer on me?"

Muttering under my breath the whole way back to the house, I pushed Gracie's stroller and finally lifted it, with her tucked safely inside, into the house.

I couldn't believe my luck when I unzipped the mosquito net and saw Gracie still fast asleep. The shower called my name, so I wheeled her into the corridor just outside the small bathroom, stripped, and turned the water to hot. Stepping under the spray once it'd warmed up, I scrubbed my skin clean and washed my hair, thinking about the dream I'd had. Why was something missing? I had everything I needed with Gracie right here. She was my world. She had to be.

Pushing the thoughts aside, I tried to think of what I'd need to do to get ready for Mason and Rick's visit. I had to get groceries, clean the house, change the sheets. *Where are they going to sleep?* Three bedrooms. Mine, Dad's and Anna's. Gracie's cot was in Anna's room, the bed still unmade in exactly the same way Anna had left it. I could sleep in there, but at the same time, I didn't know if I'd actually be able to lie down. It was Anna's room; I wasn't really ready to start clearing her stuff out. The burial had made it official—hell, seeing her on that gurney had—but the reality of her never coming home still hadn't set in. I didn't know if I was strong enough to pack her things away. I'd sleep on the sofa—that'd have to do. Mace was too tall and Rick too broad-shouldered to sleep comfortably there.

I dried myself off and dressed in shorts and a tee,

going into the living room to finish the never-ending task of folding laundry. I managed to get through the basket before I heard the telltale signs of Gracie waking up. She was cooing though, not crying, which brought an instant smile to my face. I ditched writing the grocery list and hurried over to her. Lifting her out of the stroller, I grinned at my baby girl and kissed her on the cheek. The happy little gurgle she let out lit me up from the inside, making my heart overflow. She was so damn precious.

"Hey, sleepy girl. You look like you're feeling better. I think the medicine Ford got you worked, didn't it? Let's have some playtime. Then we'll get you fed and changed, and we can go for a little road trip, hey? I've got you visiting the doc so we can get you checked out, make this sore tummy go away." Gracie reached out and gripped my little finger. "Yeah, pinky swear. I promise, I'll make it go away."

CHAPTER 6
CADEN

I stretched, cracking my back. Gracie was finally asleep, settling a lot easier after her first dose of medicine. She was in much better shape than she had been before my conversation with Ford. I needed to send him a message thanking him, but I couldn't do that while juggling Gracie. I had another load of washing to hang and a few bills to pay while she was asleep. Some of the funeral expenses still had to be paid, and then there was rent, medical bills, utilities, and Anna's lease payment on the car. They kept piling up, and my bank balance was going down. Fast. But I'd work it out. I had to.

The routine was like a never-ending hamster wheel, but it was good too. Gracie happy was a sight to behold. Her little face lit up and she got all giggly. I absolutely adored her. That girl had me completely wrapped around her finger already, and I wouldn't trade it for the world.

With a smile, I slipped on my flip-flops, did the laundry, and then sat at the small table in the kitchen that doubled as a desk and opened Anna's emails.

The knock on the door had my insides doing a cartwheel. Mace and Rick were here. I grinned as I raced to the door, though it fell when I didn't find the two men I was not-so-secretly pining after. It was Annalise's landlord—well, my landlord now that I'd changed the lease over to my name—and he didn't look happy. My high from a moment ago morphed into prickling nerves, foreboding settling over me.

"Hi, Scott. What's happenin'?"

"Caden, hi. I'm sorry, but I have to give you this. It's an eviction notice."

"It's a what?" I asked, bewildered. I hadn't done anything wrong. How the hell could he evict us?

"I know this isn't great timing. You've been through so much already, and I hate asking you to leave, but I received an offer on the place that I couldn't refuse. The house is closing in a month, so you need to be out by the twenty-second." He held out an envelope, but I couldn't get my muscles to work. My mind was telling me to rebel, and my body had just shut down.

This can't be happening. Not now, not when I'm just

starting to get used to everything. Where the hell are we supposed to go?

It wasn't fair. It wasn't okay.

The walls started closing in on me and my heart raced. I couldn't get a breath in my lungs. The room started spinning, and I wanted to fall to my knees and curse the deity who decided to fuck me over so badly in this life. I was numb all over, calm on the outside but hurtling around like a hurricane on the inside. Light-headed, I braced myself against the doorframe and sucked in a breath through my tight chest.

"No, I… fuck." I scrubbed my hand over my face and exhaled hard.

"I'm sorry. I'll, um…." He motioned to the envelope and slipped it under the mat by the door. "I'll leave you to get back to whatever you were doing."

He turned and walked back down the stairs that I'd spent so much time repairing for Annalise. I stared out, unseeing, long after his retreating form disappeared into his truck and drove away. My life was like a house of cards, collapsing into a heap before my eyes.

A wave of nausea hit me and I pushed through the door, needing to get some air in my lungs. The warmth of the sun did nothing to banish the chill permeating every cell in my body. I didn't know how much more I could take. Whoever thought up that bullshit line about whatever didn't kill you made you stronger had no fucking idea. How was I going to get us moved in just under four weeks?

I blinked when I heard my name. Mace and Rick were suddenly standing on the stoop with me. Relief swamped me, washing around me like cool ocean waters. They'd come. They were there. I wasn't alone anymore.

A sob hitched in my throat, and I was instantly engulfed by two sets of strong arms. Their warmth surrounded me, and the numbness that had seeped through me was chased away. I clung to them and cried, the uncertainty, grief and being so damn overwhelmed for so long finally having an outlet.

"That's it. Let it all go," Rick whispered in his Italian accent I loved so much, but Mace's arms, his solid strength, disappeared. Disappointment hit me like I was doused with a bucket of ice water and I shivered. I knew I was a basket case, but I just wanted him to stick around a little longer before wanting to escape. With all our history, I thought he'd cut me some slack for my meltdown, but clearly not. Rick just squeezed me tighter, showing me without any words that he'd be there for me. It might've been selfish, but I wished it were both of them.

I don't know how long he held me or how long we stood outside, but my sobs turned to hiccups and my tears finally subsided. I pulled back and Rick gave me a sad smile, his own eyes red with unshed tears. When he dried my cheeks with his thumbs, he sucked in a sharp breath.

"Hi," I whispered.

"Hi." He brushed his lips against mine and need exploded through me like a wildfire, scorching me in the best possible way. The moan that tore from the back of my throat was downright illicit. I wanted him, needed the physical release and human contact that came with a quick, dirty fuck. But he pulled back, pushing me away without letting me deepen the kiss.

He didn't want me.

Humiliated, I dropped my gaze and tried to turn away, but he didn't let me go.

Shit was just not going my way.

"Not yet, *mi carino*," he breathed against my throat as he cupped the back of my head and maneuvered me where he wanted me. I melted into his touch when he kissed a line up my neck, the rasp of his stubble and his musky scent sending me into overdrive.

His next whispered words and the brush of his lips sent shivers through me again, but for an entirely different reason. "Don't think for a second we don't want you, but we have much to talk about. We need to do that before we lose ourselves in you. And we *will* lose ourselves."

I whimpered—yes, fucking whimpered—at that. My brain was too sex-addled to understand much of what he said, but I did understand "want you" and "lose ourselves." And those two things were absolutely fine with me. I wanted Mace too, but I'd be more than happy with Rick. He wasn't second best by any means.

The hard ridge of his erection against my own had me melting into him. It was as if my body had taken over—all the shit going on in my head was too much to deal with, so it just switched off and let his touch, his words, guide me. Need and want flared hard, and I was suddenly this wanton jumble of longing.

Thoughts of Mace intruded again. He was as much a part of me as Rick, but where was he? It was confusing as fuck, wanting both, needing both to be complete. I didn't understand it, and I was too emotionally drained to resist. I couldn't fight it, kind of didn't want to either. Being there with them gave me solace. It was like coming home, and my dick—because I refused to believe it was my heart—didn't give a shit that they'd just arrived and Mace had already walked away.

"Come on, introduce me to your little one," Rick directed with a smile in his voice.

I nodded and turned away, hoping I could adjust my wayward dick, but what I saw had me freezing in my tracks: Mace with Gracie in his arms, rocking her and singing softly as he fed her a bottle. She was dressed differently to the pale purple jumpsuit she had on when I put her down, so Mace had not only picked her up but changed her, mixed her formula, and started her feed. I sucked in a sharp breath and refused to get all emotional again, but hell if it wasn't the most beautiful sight I'd seen in an age. Mace, with his muscles bunching and sexy-as-fuck beard trimmed in just the right way, looked just like Jason Statham. Holding a tiny baby in his arms while he was looking at her like she hung the moon had my heart skittering to a stop.

Then it hit me. He looked just like Jason Statham. Who was bald. And Mace nearly was too, his hair buzzed so short it was barely there. That was a change, and it was fucking hot.

"Mace," I whispered, my voice grittier than I thought possible.

He pushed through the screen door and stood in the shade cast by the house. "She was crying, so I went to her. Hope it's okay that we made friends. She's my little buddy now, aren't you, sweetheart?" He looked down at her and smiled, and then his gaze snagged mine. I so desperately wanted to go to him, but how the hell did I do that when I'd just about jumped Rick? How did I tell them that I wanted both of them without hurting either, without making them feel like they weren't enough on their own? Shit, I hadn't even officially come out to them, and there I was trying to figure out how to have both.

Then again, not coming out hadn't mattered to Rick—he'd obviously known.

Did Mace?

Rick wrapped his arms around me from behind, and I couldn't help arching into his touch when the hard ridge of his erection pressed against my ass. "He's beautiful with her, isn't he? Why don't you go greet him like you want to?"

"Because I just tried to mount you," I mumbled under my breath, but obviously loud enough that he heard.

Rick chuckled, and the sound had my dick pulsing in my shorts. I had no idea how a laugh was so sexy, but anything Rick did was. "He wants you. We both do. And I'm guessing from this"—he slid his hand down to grip my straining cock—"that you like something we're doing." The thrust of my hips into his hot hand was involuntary, and I failed miserably in biting back another moan when he added, "That's what we need to speak about, but later, yes?"

I looked him in the eye, trying to figure out if he was serious or kidding around, but seeing the encouragement was all I needed to make me move. I knew from that one look that they weren't playing me—not that I thought either of them capable of it.

Pulling away from Rick, I strode the final few steps to Mace, gripped the nape of his neck and pulled him down to me. When his soft yet firm lips met mine, it was a revelation. Different from Rick but still perfection. These two men simultaneously set me on fire and were like coming home—safe and warm, comfort and love. I didn't understand whatever it was between the three of us, but it was something real, and there was no way I'd push either of them away. Not when life had fucked me over so many times already.

I loved that there wasn't any hesitation in Mace's kiss, his tongue dueling with mine while he gave as much as he took. I wanted to get lost in him, to sink into his kiss, but I hadn't forgotten Gracie in his arms. I broke away reluctantly, but unable to leave his warmth completely, I rested my head on his shoulder, cuddling into his side. Soon I had Rick behind me again, embracing us both.

"You came. You're here." I didn't really know which one of them I spoke to, but it didn't matter. I was grateful for both of them.

"I couldn't stay away." Mace looked down, his eyes full of love as he ran his fingertips down Gracie's cheek. "I wish I knew earlier. I should've been here for you."

"We both would've been," Rick added, pressing in closer until he was wrapped around me. Blanketed front and back by them, I wanted to stay there forever. There was nothing sexual about the move; it was simply comforting—their way of showing their support, that I wasn't alone anymore.

"She's perfect," Mace whispered. "I never want to let her go."

"She is." I smiled at her and reached for her fingers. She grasped mine tight and held on. "I love her so much already. From the moment I saw her, it was like a switch flipped and bam, I was a goner."

"What about your dad? Is he coming around?" Mace asked, and I shook my head. He hadn't been home since I'd spoken to them earlier in the week. We hadn't even talked. Every time I tried calling, his cell was switched off.

"Dad's been the least of my problems, to be honest. I'm worried about him, yeah, but Gracie's been my first priority. Does it make me a bad person to let him do it his way? He's struggling more than me, but I can't juggle everything. I'm barely keeping my head above water as it is."

Rick rubbed my arms, his skin warm against my own. "It's not a competition for who's suffering more. You're both hurting, you're both grieving, and you've got a baby to care for too. I can't imagine how hard it's been on you. Don't feel bad for doing what it takes to cope."

I nodded and took Gracie from Mace. I laughed at his pout, but he need not have worried—I just wanted to show him how to burp her. When I'd demonstrated it, I handed her back and went into the kitchen to make coffee before bringing their suitcases inside. I'd lost track of what I was doing, but I didn't have it in me to deal with the bills at that point.

"You guys want a rest, shower, anything? You hungry? I haven't had much of a chance to go grocery shopping, but I have peanut butter and jelly. I could make sandwiches if you like." I was rambling, suddenly nervous in their presence. I had no idea what to do next. Did we talk? What did they expect from me? I wasn't sure how much more I could give, but whatever they wanted, I'd try. As long as they understood that Gracie would always come first, we were golden.

"Caden, come sit down. Talk to us," Rick pleaded. "What can we do to help?"

I slumped down on the old timber chair at the table in the small kitchen, relieved the focus wasn't on what they wanted from me. Sitting next to him, I smiled tentatively when he reached for my hand. Both he and Mace were being affectionate, and I loved it. Having them near was so different than cuddling with Gracie. I loved having her in my arms, but she was totally reliant on me. Being able to let go and hand someone else the reins, giving me the chance to be taken care of for just a little while, meant everything.

"I don't even know where to start. Now that Gracie's feeling better, things are a bit calmer, but shit's about to get crazy again. I've got a ton of paperwork to go through for the lawyer—Gracie's adoption papers and Anna's will and stuff. I need to sort out Anna's things—I can't keep putting that off now—and the house…." I blew out a breath. Doing any of the three most pressing things meant there was a finality to my sister's death, and I was moving on. I knew I had to, but I was scared to do it alone. "But never mind that. How was your flight?"

Ignoring my attempt at a change of subject, Mace offered, "Maybe we can do the papers for the lawyer first once Gracie falls asleep. Probably better not to keep them waiting."

"She looks tired now too," Rick added with a smile. I checked her out and sure enough, she was rubbing her eyes on her floor mat where Mace had placed her, ignoring the hanging toys.

"Wanna watch me get her sorted? She's even cuter falling asleep." The routine was one that seemed to be working for the moment, something I was grateful for given how hard it'd been to put her down only twenty-four hours earlier.

They followed me into Anna's room and I saw the quick glances between them. My sister had been gone for a month, but I still couldn't face making her bed. They didn't call me out on it, but I could almost feel the unspoken conversation between Mace and Rick, so I focused on Gracie, trying to shut them out. Putting her down on the change mat on Anna's bed, I checked her diaper and swaddled her in her wrap. I kissed her tiny forehead and lifted her to put her into her cot, but two hands on my arm stopped me. Both men had reached out and leaned in to kiss her in the same spot I had before I laid her down.

Smiling over her, I sang the only lullaby I knew. "Soft kitty, warm kitty—"

"Caden, you can't sing that to her. So lame." Rick laughed. "Let me."

Whatever he sang was in Italian, and his deep voice was soothing and mesmerizing all at the same time. Gracie fought sleep like a champion but couldn't resist when Mace ran his thumb over her temple a few times. Within moments, she'd drifted off in the quietest and calmest nap time she'd ever had.

I smiled at her once more and bit my lip, trying to school my expression. I was so incredibly lucky to have her in my life, but it was bittersweet.

Rick must've noticed my struggle, wrapping his arm around me and guiding me out. "So, tell us about this paperwork," he whispered as soon as we'd left the room.

"Before you do that, is that your room too?" Mace asked.

"What, that one?" I motioned to the room we'd just been in. When he nodded, I shook my head solemnly. "No, it was Anna's. Mine is that one." I pointed directly across the hall. "I thought you guys would stay in Dad's and my rooms, and I could sleep on the sofa."

"S'all good." Mace smiled. "We'll sort out where we're sleeping later, but you won't be on the sofa. Not when you've been sleep-deprived for weeks."

"First, paperwork," Rick steered us back to the topic he was worried about. I'd been procrastinating with it, but the sooner I had it signed and her adoption official, the sooner I would avoid risking Child Services visiting. That was all I needed.

Oh fuck, what am I waiting for? I nearly tripped over my own feet rushing to the table. Neither man questioned me, but I could see their confusion.

"Gracie's adoption papers. If I don't make it official, what if Child Services comes and takes her from me? Anna's will appointed me guardian, but they could still take her. What if her dad changes his mind?" I didn't even try to hide the panic in my voice. It was my worst nightmare come true. If losing Anna broke me, losing Gracie would kill me. "Today. I need to get it back to the lawyer today." I fumbled the papers, dropping a stack on the floor. When I reached down to pick them up, Mace stopped me with a hand on my shoulder.

"Let me, okay? Sit." Rick pulled out a chair and Mace gently pushed me into it, kneeling between my spread legs. With his hands on my knees, he looked me in the eye and promised, "You aren't alone in this anymore, okay? We won't let anything happen to her. We'll stand by you no matter what." When I blew out the breath I didn't even know I was holding, he smiled encouragingly. "Now, let's find these papers, get them signed and send them back."

I nodded, and he and Rick searched through my

semi-organized stacks. Mace sat with me and checked that I signed everywhere I had to while Rick sorted everything.

We spent hours together going through the paid bills and the outstanding ones, all the papers from the Army regarding Anna's lack of life insurance, and sorting out her estate and the utilities that still needed to be transferred to my name or canceled. It was a load off my mind at the same time as being embarrassing as hell. I was about to be homeless. These men had come halfway around the world to see me, and I didn't even have a place for us to stay after three weeks. What kind of father was I going to be if I didn't have anywhere for Gracie to sleep at night?

"Hey, you've disappeared inside your head again," Rick prodded. "What's got you worried?"

He followed me when I stood and began pacing. I couldn't hold back when he cupped my face with those strong hands, hands that could control a helicopter in some of the world's toughest terrain with ease.

The words just spilled from my lips at that point, voicing every worry. He let me speak, get everything off my chest, lending me his strength. But it wasn't just him supporting me. Mace stood behind me and wrapped his arms around my waist, pulling me back against his chest. Being in the middle of these men would, on any given day, be my fantasy come to life, but at that moment I needed more than the quick fuck I'd thought I wanted before. I needed their reassurance, their friendship, and they gave it freely.

When my words stopped and I stood exhausted between them, Rick kissed me softly. "Mace is going to put you to bed. You're going to sleep for as long as you need. I'll stay up and feed Gracie when she wakes up, get groceries ordered and do the few other things you need by tomorrow. Then, when I'm ready to sleep too, I'll join you. I respect that you don't want anyone in Anna's bed. Neither of us would take that from you."

I wanted to kiss him, and it occurred to me that he'd already kissed me in front of Mace, and I'd done the same to Mace while he was watching. It also occurred to me that I was acting like an insecure teenager.

I leaned in and brushed my lips against his with a barely-there touch, and that time he deepened it, pulling me against him and taking complete control. The touch of his hands, his lips, his tongue left me tingling. I moaned and gripped his shirt harder, rubbing myself against his leg, which was pressed between my own. Each thrust had me moving my ass against Mace's hard cock, the ridge of it making my hole clench, desperation filling me. I was a jumbled mess, but in their arms, need eclipsed everything.

"Baby, you're so keyed up. How long's it been since you've been with someone?" Rick rasped.

I couldn't breathe, couldn't think, but somehow I managed, "When I was on tour. Before everything went to shit." Mace growled at my response, squeezing my hips and grinding his dick against me. "Was thinking about both of you the whole time he blew me. Wanted you to be doing it instead of him. Wanted to be doing it to you." My blunt honesty seemed to please them, and it just made me want them more. Desire ignited through me.

"What about getting yourself off? When did you jack off last?"

I would've been mortified by his questions if there was any blood in my brain. "Before Anna." I stilled. *Before Annalise died. Before everything changed.*

There were no more words spoken, but they worked as one to piece me back together. I was guided into the bedroom I'd pointed to and they laid me down, one on either side, caressing and kissing me. Mace slipped his hand under my worn tee and I arched into his touch. Raw like an exposed nerve, I was overwhelmed and yet needed so much more. On his knees before me, Mace lifted my shirt and Rick pulled it over my head, tossing it on the floor. Bare in the warm Florida afternoon, the flat buds of my nipples pebbled, and I shuddered out a moan when Mace licked first one, then the other.

"Fuck," I hissed. "Please." I wasn't sure what I was asking for, but I needed more.

Mace obliged, undoing the button and zipper on my cargos. He tugged them open, my cock throbbing at the closeness of their hands and their mouths. God, I wanted them so badly. Soft kisses trailed down my stomach to my navel, and I moaned again, fisting the sheets. Needing to be closer to them, I reached up, touching first Mace's nearly bald head, then Rick's thick mop. A shudder ran through me as I tentatively guided them where I wanted them. A chuckle left Rick, and I gasped at the puff of warm breath directly over my cock.

"Want my mouth on your dick?" he asked.

"Please," I begged again and they obliged, pulling my cargos and underwear down together. A strong hand wrapped around my dick and leisurely pumped, making me cry out in ecstasy. I was locked up tight, and the firm grip ratcheted me up another notch, bringing me closer to an implosion of epic proportions.

"That's it, baby," Rick encouraged.

Firm lips closed over my crown and I gasped, thrusting into the warm, wet cavern. I cracked open my eyes and nearly lost it on the spot. Rick was between my legs, looking at Mace with barely contained lust as he swirled his tongue around, scrambling my brain. My body was chasing release, and I was going to come embarrassingly fast from that talented mouth.

When Mace kissed my hip and reached for my balls, cupping and tugging gently, I was a goner. I whimpered and thrust my hips forward before Rick pinched my nipple and Mace gripped me harder. I had no hope after that. The tingle that'd been a low-level buzzing before exploded through me as my orgasm hit like a tsunami. I came with a strained shout and emptied my load deep down Rick's throat.

Breathless, I floated, completely blissed out as I watched Mace pull Rick into a kiss. Their lips met, tongues tangling, and it was one of the most spectacular visions I'd ever seen. They were all masculine beauty and raw sex, and I didn't experience a single iota of jealousy. A wave of rightness washed over me, like fate had stepped in and fixed everything.

"Our first proper kiss," Mace whispered against Rick's lips with a smile. "Love the taste of you together," he moaned before Rick deepened the kiss again. I sat up slowly and ran my fingertips over their stubbled cheeks, sighing as Mace wrapped his big arm around me and pulled me closer. I rested my head against his shoulder and Rick broke away, pressing a kiss to my temple.

"I think we should have that talk now," Mace suggested, and Rick nodded. I just hummed, starting to fall asleep.

"Or maybe we should wait," he added.

"Get some sleep, Caden," Rick whispered. "We'll be here when you wake up."

"Promise?" I whispered.

His response, murmured against my temple as he kissed me and Mace curled up behind me, solidified the rightness that'd swept over me when I saw them together. "You're our man, Caden. We wouldn't be anywhere else."

CHAPTER 7
CADEN

I startled awake to a quiet house, birds chirping and what felt like a furnace surrounding me.

Blinking my eyes open, the memories from the night before flooded me: Mace and Rick caring for me and taking me to a place I'd never even dreamed of going, Rick's promise that they'd still be there in the morning, and the bodies of the two sleeping men wrapped tightly around me. It was as if they were protecting me from the world, and I loved them for it.

Gracie. Shit.

I'd been so exhausted and wrapped up in myself that I'd forgotten about my little girl.

She must be starving. Fuck, why isn't she crying?

I sprang out of bed and stumbled across the hall still naked, poking my head over her crib. She was sound asleep, peacefully wrapped in a swaddle that was done all wrong but was no less effective. Rick had stayed up with her like he'd promised. My heart tripped over itself, and I fell a little harder for both of them. Mace hadn't left my side, holding me all night like he'd done when we were on tour. I'd been so stressed that I hadn't slept properly in weeks, but he'd helped me through it then just like he'd done the night before. He was the only person I'd ever been able to fall asleep with and not have that morning-after awkwardness, even with us maintaining the façade that we were apparently straight. And Rick had kept his promise, returning to me after he'd put Gracie back to sleep.

That single night of unbroken rest made all the difference. I wasn't groggy, wasn't in such desperate need for a shot of caffeine that it had to be in the form of an IV. I was happy. I had hope, even if there were dark clouds on the horizon.

Moving into the kitchen, I turned the coffee machine on, fished out some clean clothes from the laundry room, then sat down with my coffee, relaxing for the first time since I'd left New Zealand. Then again, it wasn't so much kicking back as being content. I'd hit rock bottom, and they'd been there to pull me from its depths. I was still a mess, a definite work in progress, but for the first time in months—

probably since Mom was diagnosed—I could see light.

Gracie's grizzly cry had me jumping to prepare a bottle for her. From the note Rick had left, I calculated her last feed was nearly five hours earlier. That was far longer than she'd ever slept before, so I guessed she'd be starving.

Hurrying into her room before her cry grew too loud, I smiled over her prone form, reaching down to let her grasp my little finger. "Good morning, baby girl. You did good last night. You had a big sleep. I bet you're hungry, yeah?" Unwrapping her, I picked her up and cuddled her close. "I filled out all the forms yesterday. You know what that means? I'll be your daddy. It's you and me like I said, our little team against the world." I changed her diaper and redressed her before picking her up again.

"So, are there two more spots open on that team?" Mace asked, surprising me from the doorway. "Because I know two other guys who'd love to wear the colors."

"Why me, Mace?" I asked quietly as I sat on the bed, Gracie in my arms. I wasn't sure if I really wanted to know the answer, but it was a question I needed to ask nevertheless. Though I wasn't brave enough to face him when he answered.

There was no hesitation in his response. "Reef

said that when he met Ford, he knew there was something special about him. He couldn't walk away, even though he had everything to lose. It's the same reason why you stayed quiet about your sexuality. I've always thought of myself as straight, but I've also appreciated men as sexy. I just never thought much of it until I started spending more time with you." Mace sat on the bed, facing me, one leg crossed over the other knee. It was the one spot I couldn't look away from.

Reaching up, he cupped my cheek and pulled me in for a soft kiss that curled my toes with its sweet honesty. When he took Gracie and cuddled her to his chest, then plucked the formula from my hand and began feeding her again, I wanted to kiss him, to tell him that I'd been half in love with him for years.

"That's when I fell for you, C. I'd wanted you for months. I thought it was impossible, but then you told me you were gay, and I couldn't stop thinking about you. I didn't understand yearning until then, until I realized I wanted more than just spending time with you." He grinned wickedly at me and added, "I wanted to strip you naked and do things that a straight dude would absolutely *not* do to his friend."

I barked out a laugh at that. He'd be surprised at

how many "straight" dudes fucked their buddies or strangers to get off.

When Mace became serious again, I was captivated, hanging on his every word. "But it's not just that. I want to spend time with you and be romantic and hold your hand and shit. Do all the things boyfriends do. It's like my grand boyfriend plan." He smiled, nodding. "Yeah, the boyfriend plan. That works."

"I'd like that, Mace." I smiled back at him, shy for some inexplicable reason. "But I still don't understand why you want me."

"Because you're sexy and smart and kind and generous and strong and so many other things I admire. You pulled me in and gave me something no one else has ever given me—myself. I didn't even know who I was until you helped me discover it. And this me really likes you, on your good and bad days."

Oh God, his words. They meant everything. I had to touch him, to do something, but there were so many other questions I had that needed answering. I reached for Gracie instead and ran my thumb over her little head.

"What about Rick? Where does he fit into this grand boyfriend plan of yours?" I smirked at him, but I was deadly serious. I wanted both of them, and the small taste I had the night before confirmed how explosive our chemistry was, how right it was. I was crazy about Mace, and Rick was that perfect blend of hot, protective, and assertive that made him sexy as fuck. I wasn't ready to give either of them up, even though I hardly had them.

"You felt it at Christmas, didn't you? That day we met him? Then again during all those nights we were together at the hotel, and at the New Year's party in the club? The dance floor was packed and we could barely move, but there we were, the perfect fit together. One of the hottest things I've ever experienced was dancing with you but not touching you. It was as if we recognized each other. I was drawn to him then as much as I was you. I think you were feeling it too." He smiled when I nodded in understanding. "He's so different from each of us, and it's like he balances us. I don't ever want you to think you're not enough for me, because you are, but I need him too. Reef's words keep coming back to me for both of you. I'm going to do the same thing he did—grab on and never let go."

I had no idea what to say to him. He'd said everything right, but there were so many other things I needed to think about right then. "What do you want from me, Mace? As a boyfriend, I mean." My nerves at not being enough, not stacking up to some ideal he had in his head, were getting the best of me.

"Everything and nothing. I don't want to take anything from you, just to be there with you to experience life together. Whatever you're prepared to give, I want to give you that and more in return. It doesn't need to be complicated, but I don't want any bullshit friends-with-benefits thing either. I'm in way too deep for that."

My heart did a somersault in my chest and adrenaline coursed through me. But as perfect as his words were, the most important thing was left unspoken so far. "And Gracie?"

He didn't even hesitate. "I want to be her daddy. Well, one of them anyway."

I blew out a breath and closed my eyes, thanking the universe for not letting me fuck up my friendship with this man. I'd had enough opportunities to screw up already, and the fact that he was still next to me and so damn perfect meant everything.

"You okay, Caden?" Rick asked quietly from the doorway. I opened my eyes and nodded, not trusting my voice at that moment. "I want the same as Mace, you know. I want in on the grand boyfriend plan and the 'you and Gracie against the world' team, if you'll have me."

"You heard all that?" Mace asked, chuckling as he shook his head. "Could've helped me out."

Rick smiled and walked over to Mace, running his hand over the other man's head affectionately. "I didn't need to. You said everything perfectly. And just for the record, I felt it at Christmas too. That's why I asked you to visit me when the season ended. I wanted more time with both of you, and being together has only made me need you more." Kneeling between my spread knees, he added, "You underestimate how wonderful a man you are, Caden. Your mistake doesn't define you, and it doesn't make you a bad person. All the loss you and your father have suffered isn't karma. It's not on you."

I leaned forward into his open arms, and he continued, "If it takes me the rest of my life, I will prove to you that you're worthy of what your sister saw in you. We"—he motioned between himself and Mace—"see the same thing in you. You *are* worthy of Gracie, and you're worthy of happiness too. Give us the chance to give you that happiness. Let us love you." Pulling back, he cupped my face in both hands and looked me in the eyes. "Please, baby. It's unconventional, yes, but it's real."

"You're helping me believe it is," I whispered. "But can it work? Are we just… is it wrong? Should I even care if it is or isn't?"

"It's taken me a while to get my head around that. I struggled with what kind of person it makes me if I'm attracted to two men, but Mason understood it and worked through it with me. He helped me get to a place where I'm comfortable being me. I didn't hear what you said back to him about me, but if you feel anything for me like you might for Mason, please let me be there for you too."

I closed my eyes and leaned my forehead against his. They'd given me so much of themselves. They were putting me back together, building me back up with every word, every gesture, and I loved that they would do it for me. Being brave and telling them where I was at was the least I could do.

I looked between them and laid it all out there. "I want you both. Mace, I've been lusting over you for years, but I had no idea what kind of man you were until we spent time together. And I like him too," I added, borrowing his earlier line. I squeezed his forearm as he held Gracie. "And Rick, you made everything click into place." I ran my fingertips over his stubbly cheek. "I've been struggling with the idea of the three of us together because I don't want to give either of you up, and I didn't think I could keep you both. But I'm a pretty fucked-up mess at the moment, and I don't know if I can give you what you need. I can't even get myself and Gracie sorted out."

"From where I'm sitting, you're doing a great job," Mace supplied.

"You say that now, but you should've seen us two days ago. And there's more shit about to go down, and I have no idea where to even begin with it." I shook my head and gave voice to the thing that'd kept me up more nights than I could count. "I can't work because I want to give Gracie my complete attention, but I need a job to get by." I scrubbed my blunt nails over my scalp and groaned. "And now that I need to get a lease on a new place, it needs to happen fast." I blew out a breath, my shoulders slumping with the heavy weight of responsibility on them. "I have a bit of money saved, but it's not enough to stay home for months on end, and the one thing I thought might be good for me to do is gonna be minimum wage."

Panic rose in me, my heart beating hard and fast as it overwhelmed me. My vision swam as I thought about what struggles lay ahead with me earning next to nothing, assuming I could even get a job. My breaths quickened, coming in harsh bursts as the words tumbled from my mouth. "I've got no skills that'd earn me any decent money apart from snowboarding. That's a useless skill in Florida if ever there was one, and I'm suspended anyway, so I can't earn money from it regardless. I feel like I'm gonna drown, like I'm taking my last breath before it all becomes too much and I sink. I have no idea what to do from here. You guys are smart and successful, and I'm this washed-up mess who's about to be homeless."

My words came to an abrupt halt, my energy leaving me in a rush as the reality of my situation hit home, the humiliation of being such an abject failure looming large. I looked away from them, blinking back tears and scrubbing the others from my cheeks with the back of my hand.

I tried to stand, to lift Gracie from Mace's arms, but he held on tight to her. I understood his reticence. My soon-to-be daughter deserved the world, and at this rate, we'd be lucky to be eating ramen noodles. Mace growled, and my gut sank when Rick reached out for her and, without hesitation, Mace handed her over. They knew I was an imposter, spectacularly failing at even faking my coping skills.

Frowning, Rick cupped my cheek with his free hand and turned me to face him, concern etched on his face. "When did the landlord do this?"

"When were you planning on telling us?" Annoyance more than anything else colored Mace's tone. When I cast a glance his way, he was shaking his head in disgust and looked about ready to punch something, his hands clenched into fists and his lips pressed in a sharp line. "There are laws against kicking you out for no valid reason. We can get orders against your landlord—"

"Or you can come home with me," Rick interrupted. "Instead of staying here, the three of you could move to New Zealand. I have a big enough house, and it'd be a perfect place for Gracie to grow up. We could be her family. Everyone could have their own room. There'd be no pressure if we didn't work out. Gracie comes first, and it'd be somewhere stable. You'd have friends there and, depending on what work you're after, there are jobs too. Good schools, good child care—"

"I could look after her," Mace added, his statement sounding more like a question. "Any time with Gracie would be a dream come true for me. I'd happily look after her while you're at work."

"You can't be serious," I scoffed. "Move countries, move in with you, give Mace a babysitting job that I'd be lucky to be able to pay anything for, all in the hope that I could find a job. Believe me, I'm not that good a fuck."

I shook my head, disgust in myself bubbling to the surface. I'd fucked up. I'd been desperate to win —no, that wasn't right. I was desperate to sleep, to cope with the pressure of competing on the world stage, but I'd only managed to ruin my career and

Gracie's future. Even if I'd bombed my last season, there might've been some offers open, and instead, I'd trashed years of work, my reputation, everything. I used to think winning Olympic gold and the world championship was all I needed, but I was so wrong. Now I just needed a chance.

But that's exactly what Rick's trying to do.

I immediately regretted my outburst. He was just trying to help, and God, what a dream it would be. But I'd be taking advantage of his generosity. Mace's too. How could I accept that sort of offer without being able to give them anything in return? I'd be forever indebted to them with no way of paying them back.

Rick's house was perfect to raise a family in. Homey with a big yard, close to town and a stone's throw away from the ski fields and the airport where Rick worked. But could my pride take a blow like that? Becoming entirely reliant on him didn't sit well with me. I'd always paid my own way, always contributed, but by the time I paid for a move like that, I'd only have weeks of savings left.

Could our relationship stand it? It'd put so much pressure on us to make it work that it might be the catalyst to make everything fall apart. I was scared. There were so many things that could go wrong.

Rick stood and handed Gracie back to Mace, his

nostrils flaring as he breathed heavily. His calm voice belied the anger radiating from him. "Mason, can you please put Grace down somewhere safe."

Rick's order held an underlying steel I hadn't heard before. Shocked, I just stared at him. I knew I'd offended him, but Rick was thunderous. He clenched and unclenched his fists like he was priming for a fight, his eyes flaring with fiery passion.

He remained silent until Mace had set Gracie softly into her crib before demanding, "Out." He pointed at the door and I obliged, ready to tell him to calm down when he slammed me against the wall. Looking into his eyes, I expected to see anger, but there was disappointment instead, and it sucked the air straight out of my lungs. I'd hurt him. I hated that I'd done it, that I'd disappointed him.

He fisted my shirt and pressed me flush against the hard surface of the wall. His lips crashed down on mine mercilessly, and I opened to his assault. He was claiming me, telling me exactly who was boss, but instinct kicked in and I tried to pull away. He just held me closer, pressed into me tighter. I fought him, but my pulling away soon turned into me trying to get closer, to give as good as him.

I was outmatched and I knew it. The moment he sensed my yielding, the kiss morphed into one filled with passion and hunger as he slowly and oh-so thoroughly made love to my mouth. He fluttered his fingers over my chest up to my face and held me close, caressing me until I melted into him. Everything about him called to me, and in that moment I knew. I was in love with him. But as good as it was, there was a missing piece—Mace.

I was breathless by the time he pulled away, and as my head spun, Mace stepped into his place. He'd just stood by and watched me give in to Rick, handing over my heart to him. I needed to let Mace know that he wasn't left out from that equation. I needed him too; it wasn't just Rick I'd fallen in love with.

He could've easily overwhelmed me using his strength and size to his advantage, but Mace wasn't that kind of person. He was caring and gentle, passionate, so it didn't surprise me when he drew me into him and held me close. His warmth and the protective grip he had around me made me want to curl up in his lap. I sighed when he brushed the softest of kisses over my face and held him tighter when Rick stepped in behind me and wrapped us both in his arms.

"You're never a fuck to us, baby," Rick whispered against the nape of my neck. "You deserve happiness and love, and we want to give it to you. We want to share it with you. I'd planned on asking all of you to move to NZ with me before I left. I thought putting it out there now would give you an option. I want you both with me, but I meant what I said—it's a four-bedroom house. Everyone can have their own room. Sex is not the reason I'm suggesting this."

He blew out a breath against my skin and I shivered. I clutched them both to me, one arm on each of them as I listened to him beg me to think about it.

Mace brushed his lips over my temple, and without easing his tight hold on me, he added, "I'm asking you to trust me. I know I've broken that before and I'm so sorry, but if you let me, I'll prove I'm worthy of your trust again. And I'd never do anything to hurt Gracie. Please, trust me."

"To do what, Mace?" My voice was raw, broken.

"To love your baby girl like my own. To ask you to accept my help. I don't have to work anymore, C. I've got investments and savings and whatever else my advisor has set up. I can pretty much support myself. I don't want anything from you except yours and Gracie's time. That's it."

"Both of you, doing this for me…." I tried to express how grateful I was to them for trying to help, but nothing would come out.

Mace just tightened his hold, keeping me close and comforting me. "I'm doing it because I'm falling for you, C."

I sucked in a breath and tried to tell Mace the words I wasn't ready to say through my kiss. A slow melding of our lips, our tongues touching briefly, sending shocks of energy through me. I brushed my fingertips over his collarbone as I ran my other hand down over his belly, tracing over his six-pack.

Mace moaned and I reached back to pull Rick closer. It wasn't only Mace I wanted. It wasn't about sex though; it was comfort, forgiveness, new beginnings.

"I'm sorry for getting angry with you," Rick apologized when I broke away from Mace. Dazed and riding on cloud nine, I turned in his arms and kissed him. No less passionate, but where I'd led the kiss with Mace, I instantly yielded to Rick, letting him take control. "It killed me that you thought I'd think that of you."

"I'm sorry too," I whispered. "I knew you wouldn't use me. I was angry at myself. I fucked everything up, and for what? I've got nothing."

"We'll work something out," Mace said from behind me. "Whatever you choose, I'll do what I can to help." He looked at Rick. "I'm not choosing between you, but if Gracie needs me…."

"I get it, Mason. You don't need to explain, and, Caden, do what you've gotta do. I'll understand either way."

The resigned tone in Rick's voice broke my heart. I wanted it all, but could I have it? Could fate finally be throwing me a lifeline? Whatever happened, I didn't want us to be apart. The thought of being without them covered my sunshine with dark clouds. I'd discovered hope again in the form of these two men.

I held tighter to them, but I needed to get out and really think this through too. I needed perspective. Maybe I was rushing into it, pinning all my hopes on something that was impossible, but how would I know unless I gave it a chance? Rick and Mace had given me something pretty fundamental to think about, and even more importantly, they'd given me the option, the choice I'd been begging for.

"I can feel you tensing up." Rick's voice was quiet, soothing me as if I'd bolt if he spoke at a normal volume. "What is it? Talk to us."

"I think I just need to get out and clear my head. Maybe talk it out with my dad."

Oh shit. Dad. How could I leave him?

My heart sank. There was no way I could do it, not when he'd already lost everything. Those dark clouds rolled in and surrounded me once again. Like the callous bitch she was, fate was just taunting me, nothing more. The doorway I thought was open slammed shut in my face, forcing me to acknowledge my harsh reality.

I couldn't have a future with these men. I didn't have the option. While Dad was in Florida, I was going to have to be there too. My breath caught and I swallowed back the disappointment swamping me. I pulled away and wrapped my arms around myself, instantly missing their warmth and protection. My voice choked, I forced out, "I need to think."

Rick nodded, but concern played over his features. He must've seen something in me—although it wouldn't have been hard, as devastation had to be radiating from me.

My shoulders slumped and I turned my face away.

"Fair enough," Mace replied, ever the reasonable one. "He should have input in your decision, especially because of Gracie."

"It's not as easy as saying move in with me when we're spaced out across continents, is it?" Rick lamented.

I wished it was. I wished we had the chance, but the more I thought about it, the less convinced I was that we could make it work. It just wasn't doable. I couldn't leave Dad without any family, even if he was so distant. Especially if he was.

I couldn't bring myself to break it to Rick though.

What's the saying? Hope springs eternal? My hope had died. I thought I'd seen flashes, glimpses of it since the two men before me had walked into my life, but I was wrong. It was gone. The thought of destroying Rick's hope as well was too much. It hurt like a kick to the nuts. "I have to work some stuff out," I mumbled.

"Go, C. We'll look after Gracie. Take all the time you need. Maybe let us know in a few hours when you think you'll be back." Mace squeezed my shoulder and stepped back, putting more distance between us.

It was a pretty accurate analogy of how I saw my very near future going—the two men before me standing strong as I turned my back and walked away.

Taking those steps and walking out of the house after I'd collected my running shoes felt so much like I was saying goodbye. It killed me doing it, and I had to force myself not to look back over my shoulder.

CHAPTER 8
RICCARDO

I watched him leave, taking a piece of my heart with him.

Mason stepped close and held out his arms, waiting for me to step into his embrace. I looked at him, really took in the man before me. Physically, he was gorgeous. Tall and strong, lean muscle and a sculpted face that was far too pretty for his own good. Didn't matter what was on the outside, though—his heart was far more beautiful than any looks could ever be. I wrapped myself around him, resting my face against his shoulder. Nuzzling him, I breathed Mason in and held tight as I fought back tears.

Caden wasn't going to come to New Zealand. I knew that. Mason knew it too, and I gathered Caden did as well, if the pain radiating from him was any indication. I'd help as long as I could, as long as he'd let me. It wouldn't be easy to persuade him, especially not if what I feared came to pass. Waiting for Caden to tell us we were over before we'd even had a chance to experience "us" was like standing before the executioner.

Gracie's cry had me trying to pull away from the security of Mason's arms. "Let me get her," he whispered against my temple, and suddenly, even in his embrace, I felt very alone. He wasn't choosing her over me—I knew that logically—but it didn't help knowing that I'd be the one walking away, alone in the very near future.

"Go," I rasped, my voice thick from the lump lodged firmly in my throat. Trying to swallow around it, I pushed out of his arms and moved to the side of the corridor, allowing him to pass. When I was alone again, I looked to the front door, the direction Caden had traveled. He was long gone.

Anger, frustration, and a hell of a lot of desperation rose in me like floodwaters, threatening to drown me. I needed to do something, anything to get the emotions out before I did. A punching bag would've been ideal, weights even better, but Caden didn't have either.

Gravitating to the kitchen, I reached for the potatoes and the peeler. Cooking was a comfort for me, a reminder of the home I'd left long ago in search of adventure. Mama had passed on her nonna's family recipe for gnocchi, and I'd memorized it before I'd even hit my teens.

I tried not to slam cupboards as I looked for a pot big enough to boil water in to cook the potatoes, but I didn't succeed. Finally finding it, I yanked it out of the cabinet with more force than necessary and pressed it into the sink. White-knuckling the pot, I breathed deep and tried to cool my temper. I wasn't angry—I was powerless and scared. And knowing that terrified me even more. If I was hurting now, how bad was it going to be when this went to shit?

Taking a deep breath, I ground my teeth together and filled the pot halfway before moving it to the stove top. I returned to the potatoes, the slashes of the peeler against the white flesh of the vegetable rough and quick. When I'd peeled the entire three-pound bag, I dropped them into the boiling water and stared, watching the pot reheat and begin bubbling. I don't know how long I stood there for, but Mason's hands around my waist and the warmth of his breath against the nape of my neck had me leaning into him.

"We'll figure this out, Ricky. I know it doesn't feel like it, but we will. We came here to bring our man back, and I'll be damned if I let him walk away so easily." The strength in his voice, his conviction, made something in me unknot, but I didn't dare hope it could be true.

"I know," I whispered, my voice hitching. "But it might not be enough. Then what?"

"Then we face it together." Mason hooked a finger under my chin and turned my face to his, sincerity shining in his eyes. I fell into their comfort, my own eyes sliding closed as he brushed his lips over mine. We stood like that for what felt like eternity, me wrapped in Mason's arms as we made out right there in the kitchen until I was kiss drunk.

I blinked my eyes open and saw his warm smile, the sight lighting me up inside. Whatever happened, I knew we'd face it together. His strength gave me the courage to face whatever the future held, and I soaked it up.

"Unless you want the potatoes to disintegrate into sludge, I think they're cooked." Mason smiled before brushing his lips over mine.

"Oh shit, the potatoes." I laughed, having forgotten all about them.

"What are you making? Let me help." Mason eyed the mess I'd made, and I waved him off, moving over to collect the peelings.

"Gnocchi." I'd wanted to get in there and release some frustration, mash the shit out of the potatoes and slam pots and pans around, but the fight had seeped out of me. Now I just wanted to look after my family, to cook for them. "You can mash them if you want. I'll check on what I can make the sauce with."

"Sure." Mason grinned and I knew he was pleased. Knowing how happy I could make him just by cooling my jets had me smiling too.

"What was up with Gracie?" I asked from the dry storage pantry as I shifted canned goods around. Caden didn't even have tomatoes, so dried herbs, butter, and garlic were going to have to do.

"Just a dirty nappy. She fell asleep again as soon as I changed her."

We talked, Mason mashing the potatoes in a glass bowl and me digging the flour out of the pantry. Shifting to the refrigerator, I grumbled. It was empty. It was no wonder he'd been struggling—he hadn't even been eating.

"Damn it, Caden." I blew out a breath and closed my eyes, trying not to get upset over the empty place where food should've been. "He has nothing in here, and I need eggs."

"Let me, Ricky," Mason said quietly from behind me, grasping my hips and pulling me against him once more. "C's done the best he could. We can get groceries for him later."

"I'm not angry with him. I'm upset because it's

empty." I shook my head, turning back into Mason's strong embrace, guilt and pain overwhelming me. "He's been struggling and alone. I can't walk away knowing he's back here and might not even be eating. Bloody hell." I pressed my fingers against the bridge of my nose and breathed again. "I can't walk away."

"I know." Mason ran his fingers through my hair and kissed my forehead. "How about I get some eggs off one of the neighbors and you knead the shit outta this dough. Then when he gets back, we'll talk to him. We'll make him see."

I nodded against his chest and kissed the warm skin at the V of his polo shirt before stepping back. Mason smiled at me, then left through the front door. I slid the potato mash into the freezer and stood hopelessly in the kitchen for a moment before the urge to see the baby girl sleeping peacefully in the other room hit me.

I'd always believed parents were exaggerating when they said they fell in love with their kids at first sight. I'd thought babies grew on people, that their parents would come to love them with time. I had no doubt now that I was wrong. Seeing Gracie for the first time was enough for me to understand how powerful a parent's love was. Until Gracie, I'd never experienced an instant bond, a sudden surging of love so pure that I'd wanted to wrap her in my arms and protect her forever.

Now I understood. Now I saw exactly what that meant, what it looked and felt like.

I stood at the door, watching her tiny chest rise and fall, her beautiful eyes closed and long lashes fanning out on her cheeks, those tiny bow lips pink against her pale skin. Dressed and swaddled in a white wrap, she looked like an angel.

"Annalise," I whispered, "please make him see how much I love her. How much I love him, both of them. Please."

Disappointment hit me when there was no answer, no sign that she'd heard. Of course she hadn't. I huffed out a laugh at my ridiculousness and ran my hands through my hair, scrubbing them over my face as I sighed. When I opened my eyes, Gracie had shifted. It was as if she could read the tension rolling over me. I tiptoed into the room and leaned over her bassinet, running my fingertips over her forehead before kissing her petal-soft skin.

Standing there waiting for me was Mason, warmth in his eyes and a sad smile on his face. When he held his hand out for me to join him, I grasped it and walked with him into the kitchen where a couple of eggs lay on the countertop.

"Let's get cooking." He motioned to the ingredients I had spread out waiting for me. "You'll feel better."

I washed my hands again and got to measuring. "This is my great nonna's recipe," I explained. "Mama taught us how to make the gnocchi as kids. During the winter, we used to eat it all the time. The trick is to be gentle with the ingredients, so no kneading the shit out of this dough." I showed Mason how to fold the flour and potato together with the egg and salt, gently mixing it the whole time directly on the floured countertop.

The dough was still sticky, not yet at the right texture to roll out, when Mason nudged me out of the way. "My go." He grinned and sprinkled the remaining flour over it, then gently rolled the edges of the dough inward, using the same process I had to mix the ingredients together.

As he worked, I poked it, nodding at the improvement in its silkiness.

"*Perfetto*," I mused as he dusted dough off his fingers and moved to continue kneading. Reaching out to stop his fingers from sinking into the mixture again, I added, "No more or they'll be tough."

"Okay." He nodded. "Now what?"

"Now we roll and cut. Like this."

We worked the dough together, and I'd just slipped the final tray into the freezer when we heard a car pull up. A knot of tension coiled tight within me, and I swallowed around the lump in my throat just as Gracie started cooing.

Mason squeezed my shoulder. "We'll be okay," he assured me before walking out to see what was happening.

MASON

I refused to believe this would be the end of us. Caden walking out—literally running away, actually—just meant he needed space to think, not to work up a way to tell us that he wasn't returning to New Zealand.

I understood his worries, knew they were perfectly reasonable. I wouldn't want to leave one of my family members behind either, if I had any real family left. My parents were long gone, and my sister and I—separated by eighteen years—hadn't spoken in years. It wasn't that we disliked each other, we just had nothing in common, and the awkwardness of our conversations only grew every time we talked.

Ricky's emotions were crushing him, the fear clawing at him. He held me like a lifeline, trembling in my arms as he fought back tears of heartbreak. I held on to hope, clutching the tiny thread of possibility that held fast. As long as Caden was working through the jumble of thoughts and emotions clouded by the uncertainty that was no doubt in his head, we had a chance. I'd keep fighting for that possibility until he told me there was no hope, and probably still after that.

I kept repeating to myself that we'd get through it, that we'd come out stronger in the end. It became my mantra as I watched Caden drag his feet along the pavement away from us through the front door, and as Ricky held on to me like a life preserver.

When Gracie cried, I reluctantly released Ricky and went to her, smelling the problem before I even entered the room. It was a poo-splosion. My poor baby girl was covered in stinky goo. Cringing, I lifted her and placed her gently on the change mat Caden had set up on the bed.

"Lemmie fix you up, baby girl. It's not nice being covered in crap, is it?" Stripping her out of the dirty clothes and diaper, I wiped her down, cleaning her little body as best I could. I was a dry-heaving mess, getting more on my hands than I ever wanted to admit while I wiped away the sticky mess as thick as melted tar. And the smell. Holy shit, the smell was putrid. How could that come out of a baby's bum when all that went into her was formula? "Oh, sweet

Jesus, your shit stinks, darlin'." The cloying odor hung like a toxic gas cloud above me, but I couldn't leave Gracie on the bed while I turned on the fan to help circulate the air, hopefully straight out the open window. Where was a breeze when you needed one?

I took a moment to use some of the wipes on myself, cleaning my hands and checking my clothes. Thankfully I was poo-free, but damn, I wasn't sure if I'd ever get the stench out of my nose. I was tempted to snort some of the talcum powder stuffed in the box under the bed but resisted. Nose plugs were going to be a distinct possibility for the future though.

As soon as she was free of the mess, her eyes started drooping again, sleep overtaking her once more. She was lax in my arms by the time I'd redressed and swaddled her in the way Caden had shown me. I cuddled her close and murmured nonsense to her, watching her shift into a deeper sleep.

Laying her down in her crib, I whispered, "I love you, Gracie. Sweet dreams, my little princess."

I walked back into the kitchen to find Ricky staring blindly at boiling water on the stove and a mass of potato peelings on the countertop. He'd been slamming things around in there and now looked utterly defeated. That wouldn't do. We couldn't give up our hope. Ricky just needed to understand that I would do whatever it took to keep the four of us together. Call it blind stupidity, naiveté or stubbornness, I didn't care, but whatever happened, we would make it work.

Determination had me moving to comfort my lover. "We'll figure this out, Ricky. I know it doesn't feel like it, but we will. We came here to bring our man back, and I'll be damned if I let him walk away so easily."

It looked like one of Florida's famous storms had passed over the kitchen by the time we finished. I'd never had gnocchi before, so I had no idea whether the potato dumpling things we made would be any good or whether they'd be dense and bland. Even if they were awful, it was worth making them. I could see the tension lifting from Ricky as he worked, losing himself in a recipe that must've dated back at least a century, handed down from generation to generation. I could imagine him as a child learning how to cook the dish from his mama. She was a special lady, a spitfire who didn't take any shit from anyone. On top of that, she was a goddess in the kitchen. I adored the woman.

No wonder he was passionate about everything

he did, but especially food. It was part of him, part of his family's tradition to welcome people into their home with their warm hearts and deep food bowls.

I was handing the last tray to Ricky so he could store them in the freezer when we heard a car pull up. My man stilled, his face paling while a rock settled low in my gut. With a bravado I didn't feel, I squeezed his shoulder and reassured him. "We'll be okay," I said with as much confidence as I could muster.

Psyching myself up by repeating my new mantra over and over to myself, I pushed through the door and saw a man who could only be Caden's father. They looked alike in ways, but I didn't stop long enough to figure out exactly what they were. I needed to see Caden.

What I saw next stole the air out of my lungs.

CHAPTER 9
CADEN

The sun was already hot when I took the first steps of my run, even though it was only about nine in the morning. Palms swayed in the ocean breeze drifting off the Atlantic, the smell of salt in the air. The sky was a deep cerulean, unmarred by a single cloud.

The perfect day was a stark contrast to the turmoil surging inside me. One of the summer storms that seemed to hit more often at that time of year was predicted to roll in later in the afternoon, but at least for the next few hours, the weather was picturesque.

I started with a slow jog, my feet dragging along the pavement of the old street. The houses were beginning to look dilapidated, much like the one I was living in, but they'd soon be gone. The property developers' bulldozers would move in and the area would be gentrified—rows of architecturally designed, aesthetically pleasing townhouses and apartment buildings springing up in their place.

Anger at being a victim of capitalism instead of participating in it had me pumping my legs harder and faster. I gritted my teeth as I breathed heavily, pushing my body harder. The tree-lined avenues of old houses on big blocks of land made way for the bigger, more elaborate designs lining the canals. Manicured lawns and expensive rides were parked in garages housing entire collections of cars rather than average rides like George the Jeep. I hadn't planned on going to the marina where Dad's boat was moored, but by the time I realized where I was headed, I was already halfway there.

I crossed through the small grove of McMansions and met condos as far as the eye could see. They were identical and perfectly kept, a Florida retiree's paradise. Golf buggies and rec clubs, daily exercises along the canal-front parks within the community boundaries and a separate RV parking lot. I'd only met a few of the oldies who lived there, but the ones I'd spoken to were nice, especially the couple who leased Dad their mooring. I waved to a few familiar people as I ran, putting on a smile that those who knew me would realize was purely for show.

I was hot, the sun's rays beating down on me as my feet pounded the pavement, and I needed a drink. I'd been stewing in my own self-pity since I'd left the house an hour earlier, and I wasn't any closer to coming up with a solution. It was either Rick and Mace in New Zealand, or Dad in Florida. A far-too-long plane trip separated the two, and it was one I couldn't force upon Gracie every time I needed to get a fix of them. I was between a rock and a hard place with no way out. I'd cut my own arm off too if I saw a solution, but I was trapped. Caged in a place I didn't want to be in and mocked by what could've been.

Running along the boardwalk, I saw Dad. He'd just tossed a bucket into the cooler on deck when I stopped at his mooring. He looked up, eyes wide when he heard my heavy breathing and rasped greeting.

Shaking from the exertion, I rested my hands on my knees and resisted the urge to puke.

"Come on board, Caden. What the hell have you done to yourself?" His brows furrowed as he scrambled to help me onto his boat.

"Ran here," I gasped, flopping onto the bench seat lining the back of the cruiser. He cracked open a bottle of water and passed it to me before I could ask, and for that I was immensely grateful. Chugging it down, I closed my eyes and tilted my head up to the sky, catching my breath.

"You're lucky you caught me, I was getting ready to go fishing."

I didn't know whether to be pissed at him for being so seemingly carefree when I had what felt like the weight of the world on my shoulders, or be happy that he was doing something other than staring off into space.

"Why don't you come with me?" he asked.

I hesitated. As much as I needed the space, I couldn't be away from Gracie for that long. She was mine to care for, and Rick and Mace were already being so generous. I didn't want to take advantage of them, especially when I had news to break to them that would destroy any chance of a future between us.

I rubbed my chest, my heart hurting just thinking that.

"You okay? You don't have chest pain, do you?"

I huffed out a laugh that held no humor. "Not the kind you're thinking of, Dad. I'm fine."

He looked me over and, seemingly satisfied, he spoke again. "The tides will only be good for a couple of hours more, so we won't be out for too long. We'll be back by noon." He paused and furrowed his brow again. "Where's Grace?"

"I've got a couple of friends staying for a week or two to give me a hand. They're looking after her. Look, I dunno about going fishing—"

"I'm sure your friends wouldn't mind you spending a couple of hours away from her. They've obviously got everything under control."

Anger surged through me. "How do you know that, Dad?" I asked, my voice rising in anger. "How do you know it's all smooth sailing when you're not even around? You haven't met them, and yet you're okay with me leaving her with them for hours at a time to go out on the boat?" I shook my head as I stood to leave.

"You know why I can't come back there."

He'd always been so involved, so present, more like my best friend than an authority figure. Not that he needed to be—losing my father's respect would've been the worst thing in the world for me. I'd proved just how bad it would be to disappoint him when I was suspended. I wished I had that man back rather than the version he'd become through a shitty chain of events that would've crushed a lesser man.

I slumped back down into the seat, the fight going out of me. He moved around confidently, untying all the ropes except one and stowing them in hatches on deck. It was a sleek cruiser, but an old one in need of a bit of TLC. He'd started to fix it up, and the differences were beginning to show.

I sighed and Dad stopped what he was doing, coming to sit beside me. "You don't talk to me anymore, Dad. I wish you would. I wish…. You're missing out on so much, and I've been struggling. I'm so out of my depth. At least you've had a baby before. Gracie's been sick, and up until my friends flew in, I'd had no sleep for a week. Not even a shower because I couldn't put her down. I could've really used your help, but you weren't even answering your cell."

I shook my head and closed my eyes. He needed to hear some hard truths about how much time he spent on the boat, but he was grieving too, and it wasn't his fault that I was miserable. I needed him now though, and Gracie did too.

"Is Gracie okay?" Dad asked softly, guilt lacing his voice. I didn't want that, didn't want to upset him. Hell, I just went there to talk.

"She has reflux, so she's on medicine for it. Doc said to try it for a couple of weeks to see if she grows out of it. Sometimes it goes away pretty quickly. She slept for five hours straight last night, so she's doing better."

I looked at him then, really took him in. He'd lost weight and seemed gaunt, not the strong man I once knew. Tired eyes and lank hair that was a lot grayer too. He'd aged immeasurably in the last year. I suppose I had too. "Look, Dad, I'm sorry. I didn't mean to take out my frustration on you, but nothing seems to be going right. The landlord came over yesterday and served me with eviction papers. He's selling the house, and I have to be out in just under a month."

A horrified look crossed my dad's face, his eyes wide with alarm. "Oh shit."

"Pretty much. I can't get a lease without a job, and I don't exactly have any marketable skills to get one. I'd hoped I'd be able to stay home with Gracie longer before I needed daycare, but that looks unlikely now. I dunno if I can even afford it." I scrubbed my hands through my hair and groaned, frustration and helplessness warring within me.

"I can go back to work. We have options, we've just got to figure out what they are." When I raised an eyebrow at him, silently asking him to continue, he hesitated. "Um…."

I huffed. Yeah, that was as far as I got too. Even if Rick and Mace had given me a chance, an opportunity to make something of myself, I couldn't take them up on it.

"What else is there, son?" Dad asked, reading me like the open book I apparently was.

"I'm kinda in a relationship too." I blushed and turned away. It wasn't that I was embarrassed. I was shy—as ridiculous as that was—to admit that I'd fallen head over heels for them. But then I got a dose of reality. "But I have to end it."

"What's his name?"

I shook my head. "It doesn't matter."

"Yes, it does. You wouldn't have even mentioned you were seeing someone if he wasn't important to you." Dad paused, expectantly waiting for my answer.

"Mason and Rick. Well, Riccardo. I've been seeing both of them." I waited for Dad's reaction but he didn't flinch. He just looked at me, his expression neutral. I laughed nervously. "Nothing? Surely you have an opinion."

"What, you want me to tell you it's bad that you've fallen in love?"

I sputtered, but it was totally true. There was no denying I was in love with them. They'd seen me at my worst, they'd come when I needed them the most, and they cared for me, loved me without ever asking anything in return. I loved them. I wanted forever with them, wanted it all.

He smiled knowingly. "Don't bother to tell me you don't love them. I know that look. I saw it in the mirror many times when I thought of your mother."

I sobered thinking of Mom. "I'm sorry, Dad. Life hasn't turned out fair, has it?" I blinked back tears thinking of the happiness we'd already lost and what else I needed to give up.

"No, but you have to keep living and loving. Your mom and sister would be heartbroken if they thought for a second that you were going to throw love away. You don't just end a relationship if they're your soul mates."

Sage advice, but the old man needed to take a spoonful of his own medicine and start living again.

"No you don't, but it's complicated. Too complicated to make it work."

He shook his head and changed the subject. "How did you meet them? And do they know about each other?"

"Of course they do. I'm not cheating on one with the other. We're a trio. We're all together, the three of us." Nerves at Dad knowing I was involved in a three-way relationship plus a wave of heat hit me at the same time, thinking about what it would've been like having the two of them together, having them inside me.

Rick was a top, there was no doubt about it. Mace, I wasn't so sure about, but at a guess, I'd say I would've been the lucky bastard underneath them. I was vers and loved both, but with Mace and Rick, I would've happily bottomed for the rest of my life.

I bit back a sigh at that thought—forever. It was an impossibility, but I still wanted to swoon at the fantasy.

I looked up only to see Dad smirking at me. "What?" When he laughed and shook his head, my face flamed red.

"Tell me how you met," he prompted, and I gave in and told him. It was great finally speaking with him again, getting to see a little of the old Dad come back.

"So where do they live?"

I sighed, the question bringing me back to my shitty situation. Distance had never been an issue in the past, but I'd never had anyone besides myself to think of. Now it was going to be a fatal blow to the budding flower that our relationship could've bloomed into.

"Rick's a pilot. He flies helicopters in New Zealand. Mace was Reef Reid's coach, but when Reef retired, he took the opportunity to do the same. Mace doesn't have family tying him down, so he can move around. Rick asked us both to go to NZ with him but…." I shook my head, then realized I'd effectively told Dad my decision. I winced. I didn't want him to think he was an anchor holding me back from following them, but that's exactly how I'd made it sound. It wasn't that at all. I wouldn't abandon him. Family didn't do that.

"Ah, that's your dilemma." He nodded. "Stay with me and be a good son but struggle and be alone. Or maybe have Mace if he decides to stay with you, but be without the other person in your relationship and wear the guilt of making Mason choose you over Rick. Or you could go with them, be happy and in love and all those good things that are going to give Gracie a happy, well-adjusted childhood, but leave me behind."

I hated hearing him put it like that. He and Mom had sacrificed so much to give me the career I was desperate for and I threw it back in his face. They'd always been there for me, always encouraged me and never held me back, and now I was telling him I was feeling bad about choosing him—the man who'd already given me everything—over the men I could've spent the rest of my life loving. I was a selfish bastard.

There was no choice. Not a real one, anyway. If I could muster the balls, I knew Mace and Rick would understand. They wouldn't like it, but they'd understand. There was no way I could leave, not when Dad would be alone. How could I live my happily ever after knowing he would die lonely? And I wasn't being overly dramatic. I knew my father—he'd never be ready to date again. He and Mom had fallen in love when they were kids playing tag in their school playground. You didn't just forget that kind of love and move on. He'd never love another woman like he did her.

There was also Gracie I needed to think about. If I left, Dad would miss seeing his granddaughter grow up, and I'd deprive her of her pop. I couldn't do that, couldn't take Gracie from him too, not when she was the brightest spark in our lives after so much misery.

I had no option, but my heart still shattered into a million pieces at the thought of ending things with them. I loved Mace too much to ask him to stay. He should go and be happy with Rick. They'd have a good life together.

My shoulders slumped, and I nodded. "It's gonna be hard to say goodbye to them, but I have to."

"I think we should talk this out as a family," Dad replied thoughtfully. "How about we forget about fishing and head home?" I looked at him confused—*family?*—and he added, "It's pretty clear that you're in love with those boys, and you trust them enough to look after Gracie. That makes them family, don't you think?" Without waiting for me to answer, he continued, "Come on, it's time I started acting like a father and grandfather again." He began pulling the mooring ropes out of the hatches again, tying the boat in place so it couldn't float away or smash against the pylons holding up the jetty in a storm.

I was quiet the whole time he worked, and once he'd finished, I followed as he led me to his truck and drove us home.

When he pulled in the drive, I looked out without moving and said, "I filled out the adoption papers yesterday. The lawyer is getting the paperwork processed, and once the judge signs off on it, I'll be Gracie's dad. What if I fuck it up, Dad? What if I'm terrible on top of being a complete screw-up at everything else?"

"Caden, you're not a screw-up. You make me proud every day. You put everyone else first, take the weight of the world on your shoulders, and you're a good man. A good father. Even now, when a lifetime of your happiness is at stake, you're prepared to walk away from it to protect me." He squeezed my shoulder and opened the door. "But if you do that, when are you going to live for you?"

His words hit hard, resonating deep within me, in that part of me that longed for what he wanted me to have, what I wanted to have. But I couldn't seize my own happiness, not at my father's expense. He had no one. He'd sacrificed so much for me so I could achieve my dreams; I couldn't repay him by walking away when he needed me most. Sometimes another person's happiness—especially if they were family—was worth more than your own. Wasn't it?

"You'd do it for me. It's what family does for each other."

CHAPTER 10
CADEN

I sounded miserable even to my own ears. Dad just shook his head at me, disappointment coloring his features as he climbed out, waiting for me when he reached the top of the stairs. I followed him slowly, each step one closer to breaking the hearts of the two men who owned mine.

Mace strode out of the house, meeting Dad at the top of the stairs, but he barely paused before taking the small flight in two bounds and coming to me. "No," he whispered when he got closer. "Please don't do this." He tried to wrap his arm around me, but basking in the love he was only too willing to give would make what I had to do impossible.

I shook my head and moved away from him, trying to keep him at arm's length as I steeled myself and walked up the stairs, only to meet Rick's gaze head-on. I had to look away; it eviscerated me seeing the devastation clouding his features. A storm was brewing in his eyes, and all I could do was pray I had the strength to walk away when it came to the crunch. It was the last thing I wanted, but I had to put my family first.

I watched as Dad clapped Rick on the shoulder and walked inside. When I passed Rick on the stairs, he wouldn't look at me. I deserved it, but it still tied me in knots knowing I was going to hurt him as badly as it was hurting me.

Dad went straight to Gracie and picked her up, holding her close to his face and talking to her with a smile tilting his lips. It was effortless for him; he knew exactly what to do with her.

I smiled at her and kissed her mostly bald head. "Hey, baby girl. I'm back."

He smiled sadly at me. "You should refer to yourself as Daddy or whatever you want her to call you. That way she makes the connection early and will start to call you that. It's one of the proudest moments in your life to hear your baby say your name for the first time. I'll never forget the first time you called me Dada."

Dad smiled at me, and once the other men walked inside, he motioned to the table. We sat as he laid Gracie on her blanket under the hanging mobile so she could play with the toys. "I'm calling a family meeting to discuss this situation."

"Sir—" Mace started.

Dad held up his hand and cut him off. "My father was Sir, and I hated calling the miserable bastard that. It's Gabe, please. I think we've met before. You're Mason, right?" After introducing himself to Rick, Dad got right to the point. "Caden came to see me this morning. He told me the three of you have started seeing each other. He also hinted that you've asked him and Gracie to move to Queenstown with you both. He's worried about leaving me here alone, probably picturing me dying a lonely old man. Am I right?" When I nodded, he shook his head and huffed, clearly exasperated with me. "Caden, what are you going to do if you stay in the US? And where in the country are you thinking of living?"

I shrugged, not looking up. "Here, I suppose. You've got your boat, so being near the water is kind of important to you. I figure I'll pick up whatever work I can find."

"And where will you live?" he prodded. I shook my head and raised my shoulders again. I had no idea. "Right. And Rick, Mace, what exactly were you boys suggesting to my son?"

"I've got a decent-sized house. He and Gracie could each have a bedroom, and Mace and I could take the other two. I want to be in a relationship, but I'm not going to pressure Caden into it, and I don't want him to think my offer is conditional on us being together. I just want to be a part of Gracie's life growing up."

Mace chipped in then, and I knew I was going to go to hell for doing what I had to do. "I offered to watch Gracie while Caden works. I'm retired, so I don't have any work commitments. I didn't want to get paid for it, I just wanted to help too."

"What are your intentions with my son?" Dad asked with a straight face, but I wasn't sure how. It was the most un-Dad-like thing I'd ever heard him say. When I started protesting, telling him he didn't need to know that, he shushed me with an annoyed glance and motioned for them to explain.

Rick didn't hesitate. "Long term, I want the three of us as partners and Gracie as our daughter."

Dad smiled. "Good answer. Okay, Caden, you need to make up your own mind on this, but I'll tell you something, and you need to listen and listen hard. You cannot live for everyone else. If you're sad and lonely, Gracie will suffer too. Be happy and she will be too. It's not enough to survive, you should thrive. It's what you deserve. You three also need to be honest with each other. I didn't tell Annalise how much I loved her before she went in to have Gracie, and now I'll never get the chance. Don't make my mistake. Life is far too short for that." Dad stood and busied himself, moving around some of the papers on the table to clear a space. "Caden, I need to borrow your tablet for a while, and I work better when it's quiet, so if you three could make yourselves scarce—perhaps talk things out in another room—that'd be great."

I was being dismissed, with no idea what was going on.

"I thought we were having a family meeting? Or was that it, because our family meetings used to include a hell of a lot more discussion rather than you giving me some advice that still doesn't change anything for me."

"I'm happy to talk it out when you're not being so shortsighted. Until then, scoot. I need to look up how to immigrate to New Zealand."

"What?" I asked, confused. *What is he talking about?*

"Well, if I move with you so I don't die a miserable, old, lonely man, will you go to Queenstown with Mason and Rick?"

It was like a lighthouse's candle switched on, illuminating the rocky path in a brilliant white light. Never in a million years did I think Dad would even consider leaving the US.

"Stop looking at me like I've grown two heads," he chastised, then, becoming more serious, added, "Maybe it's time we both had a change of scenery. Your mom and sister would understand. We don't need to visit the places we scattered their ashes to be with them—we carry them in our hearts. If my coming with you will give you a lifetime of happiness anything close to what your mother and I shared, how can I deny my son and his daughter that?" He grasped my arms and implored, "If you were in my position, would you do it for Gracie?" When I nodded, he smiled. "Then you understand when I say I need to do it for both of you. It's my privilege as a doting grampy."

I stood from the chair slowly and stepped into his arms, hugging him hard. The only words that formed, that I could force out from my tight throat, were "I love you."

"Tell those boys you love them too, Caden. Tell them every chance you get." He clapped me on the back a couple of times and stepped away, waving us off when he spotted my tablet lying half under a pile of junk mail.

I think I was in shock. My mind usually went a million miles a minute, but it'd come to a screeching halt and was utterly blank. Nothing, no words formed. I stood there frozen in a daze like I was disconnected from my body.

"Gabe, thank you. It means the world that you'd consider doing this for us." Mace wrapped an arm around me and I melted into his side. His warmth injected life into me again like he and Rick had always managed to do.

Rick was at my other side but didn't reach for me. Instead, he held his hand out to Dad, pulling him into a hug and kissing both his cheeks. "This is what we do in my family. Thank you for including Mason and me in yours." When he focused his attention on me, the remnants of that moment of frozen shock were wiped away. "Let's go talk privately. I think we have much to say." Taking me by the hand, Rick guided us into the bedroom and went to close the door.

"I need a shower," I blurted out. "I went for a run. I... I probably stink." Apparently, my brain had reengaged in stupid mode. I closed my eyes and shook my head, giving myself a mental slap. The others laughed and wrapped me up tight.

Rick spoke, his voice husky. "We can shower, but first I need to know—"

"I lied to you guys," Mace interrupted. Rick went still in my arms, and I must've had a bruising grip on Mace because he grasped my hand and put a little distance between us. "I told you the other day that I was falling for you, but that's not true." Mace paused and took a deep breath while my insides went into free fall like I'd been thrown out of a plane. "I'm already there. I'm in love with both of you."

He blew out his breath and visibly braced himself for our reactions. I didn't think, just moved, throwing myself against him and practically climbing him like a tree. Rick wrapped his arms around me from behind and held tight.

"Me too. I love you too, Mace." I kissed him again before turning and brushing my lips over Rick's. "I love you too, Rick. Both of you. I didn't want to hurt you. It was killing me, but I couldn't leave Dad alone. He's lost so much too. I couldn't do it to him."

"We need to communicate more. For three pretty smart dudes, we're hopeless at it," Mace chuckled.

"Promise me you're all in, Caden, that you'll work on *us*." Rick's voice was quiet, full of pleading, and I couldn't resist him. I didn't even want to try. "I love you both too much to lose you." My heart skidded to a stop again and then sped up, doing triple backflips and spins midair like I used to do on the slopes.

"I'm in. I want this more than I've ever wanted anything else before." I motioned between us. "I want us to be a family."

"Let's go take a shower. I wanna get all dirty with you." I laughed at Mace's comment while Rick let out a sound halfway between a growl and a moan. I couldn't wait to hear what other sounds we could get him to make.

We dashed up the corridor, probably sounding like a herd of elephants, but I was riding a high, my heart light for the first time in over a year. Joy filtered through me. Hope buoyed me. Love wrapped around me like a warm blanket.

Between them, I was invincible.

The shower was far too small for three grown men to fit into, so we took it in turns. Ten of the longest minutes later, I'd watched Mace and Rick run soapy hands over themselves, teasing the ever-loving fuck out of me. It was sweet revenge watching their nostrils flare and Rick lick his lips as my fingers circled around the base of my cock and I stroked myself while the hot water cascaded over my shoulders. Mace's pupils were blown, lust hardening his already solid body.

Empowered, desired, emboldened, I switched positions and stuck my ass out, rubbing my soaped-up fingers along my crease and down to my hole. Spreading my cheeks so they could see what I was doing, I dipped my fingertip inside, clenching my pucker tight around it. My cock was leaking, my channel throbbing with an emptiness that needed to be filled. Fuck, I'd just about kill to get inside either one of them, but I was going to have the time of my life being a needy bottom to those two.

I couldn't wait any longer. After rinsing all the soap off, I turned the faucet off, grabbed a towel and dried myself in quick, uncaring swipes. My only priority at that moment was getting my men horizontal, preferably in a position that I could have both of them.

Rick laughed, the sound coming out raspy and strained. "Looks like our man has made a decision."

"Yeah, I want you to nail me into the fucking bed." My towel covering the bits that Dad wouldn't want to see if he happened down the corridor at that moment, I led the charge back to my room before either could respond.

Rick was close on my heels but Mace lagged behind, seemingly hesitating. I got it. Sex was a big deal when it was with a man for the first time. He'd been with women in the past—none of us were virgins—but this was different. On top of the mechanics, there was the emotion to contend with too. I certainly hadn't experienced anything like it before, so I understood if it was nerves he was dealing with.

I cupped Mace's face and brought his mouth to

mine in a slow kiss filled with promise. "We go as fast or slow as you want. We only do what you're ready for. If you want to stop at any time, that's okay, and we don't even have to have anal. If you're not feeling it, there are plenty of ways we can still be together."

"It's not that," he replied. I didn't miss the fact that he wouldn't look at me, and he was fidgeting like he was nervous. "I... when I think about us together, you're inside me, not the other way around." He blew out a breath and shook his head. "I know you're probably thinking I'm a disappointment—"

I gripped my dick tight around its base to stop the rush of my orgasm barreling through me. The thought that Mace would want to bottom was so fucking hot that it had me desperate to take him to heaven with me.

"Oh, baby, you're no disappointment," Rick responded, moving to stand behind Mace. "You feel this?" I watched as Rick ground against Mace's ass and Mace's eyes rolled back in his head, arching his back as he tried to get closer. I was jealous of Rick's cock pressing against that tight ass for a moment, until I remembered that it'd be lodged deep in me before long. "I will be inside you sometime soon, and I can't wait. But this time, I think Caden wants you.

Look at him, Mace. You almost made him come just by saying you wanted to give yourself to him. Damn, our man's hot when he's desperate to fuck, isn't he?"

The strangled moan, which sounded like a whimper even though it totally wasn't, ripped from my throat and the hand I had strangling my dick began stroking. Precum leaking from my slit lubed my way, and a full-body shudder ripped through me. I needed to slow down, but fuck, I wanted him so bad. "Need to be inside you, Mace."

He climbed on the bed and spread his legs, offering himself up for us. Long, strong legs splayed wide, his balls hung low and his cock lay rigid against his six-pack. His happy trail was starting to gray, just like his beard, and I was digging the silver fox look. But it was his eyes, blazing with passion, that had me riveted. He was a wet dream, so damn potent, so addictive.

Mace rubbed his hand along his thigh in a move I was sure he didn't even realize was sexy as hell. I turned to Rick and knew from his look that he was just as determined to make it good for Mace as I was.

I wanted to make a meal out of him.

Together we climbed on the bed, having lost our towels the moment the door shut behind us, and we crawled over him. Rick started at his ankle, his tongue tickling the sensitive skin there while I went for his mouth. Kissing, licking and nipping down his throat, I breathed deep, filling my lungs with the scent of the man I loved.

Pausing, I shuffled down the bed a bit. I needed a taste of my other man. I kissed Rick's shoulder as he nibbled on the inside of Mace's thigh, moving higher with every sensual bite until he turned his attention to me and slammed our mouths together. Our tongues dueled, lips sliding together like they'd been made to kiss like that forever. And maybe they were. Now that I had them, I wasn't letting either of them go.

I broke away and watched Mace. Seeing him stare at Rick and me hungrily was an aphrodisiac of the most intoxicating kind. Everything either one of them did turned me inside out.

I descended on Mace again, kissing him like he was the oxygen I needed to breathe. When he let out an indecent moan while his mouth was pressed to mine, I guessed that Rick had deep-throated him.

"Motherfuck," he gasped when I pulled back to watch Rick take him down to the root, pressing his nose into Mace's pubes. I wanted in on the action, needing to taste him too. Nudging Rick's shoulders, he moved to make room for me. Mace's long muscular legs surrounded me, vibrating with need as he thrust into Rick's mouth. I dove straight for the soft skin of his sac, teasing and tasting him. The faintest taste of soap and clean skin swept across my taste buds and had me desperate for more.

I licked him, dragging my tongue over his almost hairless balls. I hummed in appreciation, loving the feel of him writhing beneath me. I took one of his testicles into my mouth, Mace arching up at the dual attack on his senses. His legs scrambling for purchase and his hands fisting the sheets, he was a sight to behold. And I was like a drug addict getting his high, needing it. I moaned as I breathed in that unmistakable scent of man and sex and Mace, running my tongue over his balls again. Mace cried out, his body locking up tight. He was right there on the cusp, ready to shatter, but Rick denied him, pulling off at the last possible second. Edging was sweet torture, and by the pained howl Mace let loose, I guessed he hadn't partaken in much of it before.

This is gonna be fun.

"Our man likes that, Caden. You think he'd like some rimming too?"

"Oh hell yeah," I breathed, moving my mouth down.

"What the hell?" Mace tried to twist away from me and I pulled back, ready to stop, but Rick's strong arms held him in place.

"He'll stop if you hate it, but would you try it for

us? It's unlike anything you've ever experienced before. I'm not one for ass play, but even I fucking love it." Rick's words were gentle, handing the reins over to Mace, exactly as it needed to be in that moment. "I can do it to Caden first to show you, if you'd prefer."

"No, I trust you guys. If you think I'll enjoy it, I'm in. You just shocked me, that's all." Mace's tone was apologetic, but he needn't have been worried. Whatever he was willing to give, I'd grasp with both hands.

Rick gently held his cheeks open, and Mace widened his legs for me. "You've got such a pretty hole, Mace. Can't wait to fill you up. Can't wait to taste you." His hole clenched tight. I wasn't sure if it was embarrassment or lust causing the move, but either way, I loved it.

I moved closer and licked from his crack to his balls and Mace shouted out, making me hum against his skin. I loved rimming, both giving and receiving. I didn't do it often—that kind of gymnastics in the places I traditionally had sex was pretty much out of the question—but when I did, getting a reaction like Mace's was a shot of adrenaline straight into my bloodstream. I dove in, licking and nipping him.

The touch of Rick's tongue against the crease where my ass met the back of my leg had me instantly moving, spreading my legs like the greedy son of a bitch I was. Long, teasing swipes in every place except my pucker had me groaning and wiggling around, trying to get Rick where I needed him most—as if he didn't already know. I was going insane, mindless with lust with his tormenting.

Mace was the perfect distraction for me, his ass tempting me to go to town on him. I wanted to dive in and give him everything, but I knew I needed to hold back a bit, at least for now. Touching my mouth against him, I savored his natural spice and used my lips and tongue to soften his clenching muscle, readying him for my fingers. All the while my cock was leaking onto the sheets, my ass up in the air begging Rick to fill it.

Mace's choked cries of pleasure had me pushing his comfort zone further, trying to take him to nirvana. Wetting a finger and coating saliva over his hole, I eased my fingertip into him. Mace hissed and I paused, breathing through the loss of Rick's mouth on my perineum. He tossed me the lube from my nightstand drawer and I smiled wickedly.

This is going to be so much fun.

I coated my fingers in slick and drizzled more onto Mace's entrance before pushing back in, a little deeper that time. I stilled, letting him get used to the intrusion, and Rick did the same to me, prodding me open with just a fingertip. I slowly pumped my finger in and out, my touch gentle until Mace was pushing back against me, letting me know he was ready to take a second finger.

I rode Rick's digits, lodged deep in my ass, angling my hips to get him to hit my prostate. But it didn't happen. Every time I changed the tilt of my pelvis, Rick moved his fingers, staying away from the one place I needed him. But the push and pull around the bundle of nerves centered at my opening were sending me into hyperspace nonetheless. Shamelessly, I chased the orgasm I so desperately wanted, fucking myself on his hand. At the same time though, I didn't want to come. Mace's ass was begging to be filled, and I wanted to lodge myself to the hilt in my man. Before I could do that though, I needed him to understand just how good it could be.

I brushed across his prostate and he gasped out an "Oh, fuck."

My laugh was strained, turning into a moan when Rick mirrored it on me.

"Again," Mace begged. The litany of curses, moans, and gasps that erupted from him when I pummeled his P-spot and the snap of his hips as he impaled himself over and over on my fingers had me reaching for my cock, trying to stop my own orgasm.

Rick batted my hand away, rolling a condom over

my length. "Make him come and I'll fuck you into the sheets like you wanted, baby. And if you're lucky, he'll ask you to fuck him."

That was more than enough motivation for me.

I sucked Mace to the back of my throat and added a third finger, applying just the right pressure to his prostate to make him erupt. His body locked tight under me, his hole strangling my fingers as his channel clamped tight around my digits. His back arched, head pressing into the pillow, and the corded muscles along his throat and chest stood out in stark relief. A sheen of sweat broke out over him, and in the dappled light of the bedroom, it was one of the sexiest sights I'd ever laid eyes on. Hands holding the sheets in a white-knuckled grip, he choked out a breath as he emptied himself down my throat. There was no pulsing of his cock, no spurts, just a rushing that had me swallowing more than once to capture all his essence.

When it finally subsided, Mace slumped, going lax on the bed. His pale skin was a beautiful contrast to the dark gray sheets, and I wanted nothing more than to do it all again. My neglected dick, which was harder than an iron rod, twitched between my legs. The next time, if my luck held, would be with my cock rather than my fingers. And if I was really fucking lucky, Rick would move his fingers—or perhaps remove them and slide that thick veiny dick deep inside me.

"Fuck me." Mace huffed out a laugh.

I moaned, burying my face along the crease of his leg as Rick pulled his fingers from my channel to taunt me, rubbing the head of his cock over my hole.

"Please," I begged. "Rick, I need you inside me."

He pressed into me agonizingly slowly, holding my hips steady so I couldn't force him to go faster. I choked out a cry and fisted the sheets below Mace. God, he was so thick, a damn tree trunk all up inside me, but fuck, he knew just how to move. Slow, sensual pumps of his hips had my toes curling. The sounds coming out of me were incoherent, a jumbled mess of grunts, moans, sighs, and begging. I wanted hard, but this was so much... more. When Rick bent, pressing his front against my back before licking and biting down on the nape of my neck, I nearly lost it.

"Ricky, hold tight for a sec," Mace interrupted. He shifted and I lost my pillow. I cried out, devastated at the loss, but when Mace slid farther down the bed, spreading his legs wider and cradling my whole body, I sank into his embrace. "Come inside me, C," he whispered in the sexiest rasp. "I need you."

The shock of his comment brought me back into myself, and I whimpered as Rick hummed and stroked my cock with his slippery hand. Fumbling, I tried to line myself up, but it wouldn't work. *Why can't I get in?* Suddenly Mace's legs were up around my shoulders and his hole was right there, right at my cockhead.

I couldn't wait, couldn't do patient that time around. I tried to make it good for Mace, holding back as much as I could, but I still probably went too fast, pushing past his tight ring and burying myself to the hilt in one stroke. The column of muscles cording in Mace's throat as he strained, struggling to get used to my intrusion, had me trying to get closer to him, to soothe him. I wanted everything from them, needed to give them every part of me too.

"God, you're so tight," I gasped. "I can't last long."

"Move," Mace demanded, one hand pulling Rick's face to his for the dirtiest fucking kiss I'd ever seen and the other jacking his cock between us. He was hard, and not just like an "eh, I'm bored so I'll whack one out" type boner but a "I haven't touched my dick in a month and I could hammer nails with it" one. I leaned in closer and licked along the seam of their joined mouths, sliding my tongue between them while I pushed back against Rick and slid out of Mace nearly all the way.

Our kiss was messy and our rhythm off, but at that moment, something settled in me and I didn't want to race to the finish line anymore. I wanted to fly, to flip and spin, to soar. I used to do it over fields of white snow, but at that moment, I was doing it with my men, the two loves of my life.

We made love, following the music in our heads playing just for us. We moved and touched, caressed and loved every inch of each other we could reach, and when I did finally come with a cry muffled in Mace's throat, my guys were right there with me, Rick pulsing inside the sheath separating us and Mace's cum spilling between us after a few extra strokes of his cock.

Sweaty and breathing hard, we tumbled onto the bed, Rick stripping off both his and my condoms and tossing them aside. Tangled limbs and slow kisses with first Mace and then Rick had me burrowing in closer. I never wanted to move.

"Neither do I," Mace murmured. I hadn't even realized I'd spoken it out loud, but knowing he shared my sentiment made me smile. "I didn't know it could be that good," he added. Rick hummed in agreement, and I brushed my fingers over Mace's chest and down to the drying cum on his belly, rubbing it around. They surrounded me, and it was fucking glorious. "I want to do that again. At least twice a day. Forever," Mace sighed.

"You want to try being inside me?" I asked, a little

curious as I moved my hand lower, playing with the hair of his happy trail. I couldn't stop touching him. It wasn't sexual, simply comforting. A reassurance that he was right there with me, and we'd moved past friends into something so much more. I cupped his flaccid cock and balls, just stroking the soft skin in my hands. Mace hummed and Rick chubbed up behind me, his dick lengthening as he pressed against my cheeks. Mace widened his legs and I slid my hand lower, caressing his perineum and around his hole. It was still a little open, so I slid my finger inside. I was checking him for tearing but fuck, it was arousing as hell watching him get instantly turned on. My man was a slutty bottom, and I loved him for it.

"No," he breathed.

I froze, panic surging through me. *I wasn't gentle enough. I hurt him. He hated it.* Every worst-case scenario ran through my head as I withdrew my finger.

"Don't stop," Mace demanded indignantly before pulling me down to him for a kiss that melted my brain. I pumped my finger in him again without even knowing what I was doing, seeking his prostate. It was swollen, but he jerked in my arms, riding my digit. Mace's breathing picked up and he moaned. The heated silky slide of his channel had my dick jealous of my finger, but I wouldn't be in him again that day, not without hurting him. I dry humped his leg, rocking my steely erection against him, seeking out whatever friction I could. Rick was doing the same to me, rubbing his cock against my ass, making me desperate.

"I don't wanna be in you, not when it feels like this for you to have me. Fuck, I wanna come again, but I won't get it up," Mace gasped.

"Oh, baby, you have a lot to learn," Rick groaned, his voice full of lust. "Caden, suit me up and ride me. Mason, sit on my face. I wanna suck your cock."

I scrambled up as soon as Rick moved onto his back, rolling on the condom and slathering him in another coating of lube before I sank down onto him. The stretch, the tight fullness was so damn perfect. He was thick and veiny, uncut and pulsing inside me. I moaned and rocked on him tentatively, tagging my P-spot as I slid back down on him. My eyes closed, I lifted again, relishing the pull of his shaft out of my channel before slamming back down on him.

Choking out a cry, I reached for him to balance me and got Mace's hips instead. I opened my eyes and saw Mace sinking his still-soft dick into Rick's mouth. His hole winked at me, clenching as it begged me to fill him again. Not even the most well-hung porn star's cock could reach the distance, so my fingers, my tongue would have to do. I leaned forward, licking the reddened skin before gently sliding my middle finger in. He rocked onto my digit, shameless as he chased the orgasm that Rick and I would give him.

As I massaged his prostate, he bucked against me. "Fuck, keep doing that. I'm gonna come again."

I worked my own cock and forced myself to hold still while Rick slammed into me hard and fast. I fingered Mace, eating him out like a starving man at a buffet. We were frantic, chasing another release. It was as if our first round, and second for Mace, only whet our appetites for more. Heavy moans and grunts filled the room when Rick tagged my prostate in just the right way again, and I sank my finger into Mace's ass, licking around his rim.

My ass clenched tight, my release hitting me like a Mack truck. It started in my pelvis and radiated outward, sending tingles through my balls and up my cock, down my legs and through my body. Even my fingers were electrified, my nerves buzzing with the strength of my release. I shouted out, unable to control the all-consuming ecstasy ripping through me as I unloaded all over Rick's ripped abs. A muffled shout penetrated my overwhelmed senses and Rick slammed deep in me once more. His swelling cock stretched me farther, sending another shot of adrenaline through me and more cum spilling out of me.

Whimpers sounded from Mace as he writhed on my finger. I hadn't realized I'd stopped moving, stopped licking him. I added a second finger and pumped in and out, zeroing in on the bundle of nerves buried in him. He had no chance between our combined efforts, his body locking tight on a silent scream as his orgasm charged through him.

He collapsed onto the bed at a ninety-degree angle to us, his leg still sprawled across Rick's chest. I fell the other way and cuddled into Rick's side while Mace recovered.

When his breathing had slowed, he threw his arm across his face. "I dunno what that was, but you can do it to me any day."

"Prostate orgasm," I mumbled, sleep beckoning me as my eyelids grew heavy.

"I'm wrecked," Rick groaned. "Think we can nap for a bit?"

I didn't bother answering him, just laid my head on his shoulder and closed my eyes. Mace jostled us a little when he shifted, and I smiled when he grasped the hand I had rested on Rick's chest, intertwining our fingers. I drifted quickly, filled with hope for what the future would hold for Gracie and me.

CHAPTER 11
CADEN

Gracie's cry startled me, especially since it came from outside.

Shit.

I scrambled up, falling over my own feet as I tore out of the room, cursing the closed door in the way. Charging through the house, my heart beating furiously, I stopped short when I saw Dad outside with her, picking her up out of her stroller. With a sad smile on his face, he bent and kissed her little head and popped the cap off the bottle one-handed. Her little lungs worked well, and by the time he'd gotten himself comfortable on the park bench under the big orange tree in the yard, she was screaming the neighborhood down. I saw, rather than heard, his lips moving as he talked to her, and I closed my eyes, sending up a thank-you to Mom and Anna for finally making him see. We had a long way to go, but I knew if we stuck together—all five of us—we'd be okay.

"He looks happy holding her, doesn't he?" Rick said from my side, making me jump. He reached out, brushing his fingers against my hand, and I leaned into the contact, swooning at the warmth that spread through me from his touch. "I'm so glad you went to him."

"So am I." I nodded. "Never in a million years did I think he'd volunteer to leave the States."

Mace sidled up between us, wrapping his big arms around each of our shoulders. "He's doing it for you and Gracie. I respect that."

As if he knew we were speaking about him, Dad looked up and called out, "If you boys are awake and decent, I've got some thoughts on how we go forward."

"Okay, Dad. Give us a minute. We'll come out." Looking down at Mace and Rick, I saw they both were as naked as me. Grinning, I motioned to the bedroom. Once we were dressed and sitting around the tree with Dad and Gracie, Dad began explaining.

"My engineering background means I qualify for a visa. My skills are in high demand, so I shouldn't have a problem getting over. Mason, I don't know much about your background, but I'm assuming as a former coach, we should be able to get you a visa."

When he paused, Mace nodded. "I spoke to an immigration lawyer while I was on vacation. She's got the paperwork ready, so as soon as I give her the go-ahead, she'll get it submitted."

"Great." Dad paused again and turned away. I knew that move. He wanted to say something but was nervous about doing it. I wasn't sure if I wanted to know, but Dad persisted, blurting out, "Son, as far as I can see, you're the only issue. Your best chance is to have a shotgun wedding with one of these two and go over as their spouse."

I opened my mouth and then closed it again, speechless as I looked to Rick for help. Surely he understood that I'd want to get over there on my own merit. Or maybe not. Knowing my overprotective… boyfriend? Partner? Lover? Whatever he was, he'd want me there as quickly as possible.

Rick smirked and I laughed nervously. "He could come over on a holiday visa, spend a few more months at home with Gracie like he wanted to. Then when he's ready to work, he could apply for a job and swap over to a work visa. It's exactly what I did when I moved over there," Rick explained. "And given Mace will be home too, you won't have to wait for a childcare place to become available for Gracie once you do get the visa and start your job."

"Yeah, let's do that." I nodded a little too vigorously, making the others grin and Mace wrap a protective arm around me.

"Baby, you know you'll wear our ring one day, don't you?"

"Gimme a little longer than twenty-four hours after our first kiss to do that though, okay, Rick?"

Dad's chuckle had us all laughing.

Sobering, Rick asked, "When are you thinking you'll try to come out?" He pulled at a blade of grass on the lawn, tearing it up. "Will you have to wait until Gracie's adoption is final?"

"We do, but it's a straightforward application. Anna's will was clear, and she had all the paperwork from that dickhead sperm donor relinquishing parental rights signed well before Gracie was born. The lawyer was confident that it'll be turned around in a few weeks rather than months. Then it's a matter of getting an updated birth certificate and passport." I counted it out in my head. "I'd give it three months, maybe."

He breathed out in a gush, his shoulders sagging. "Oh."

"Mace is gonna come earlier than that," I volunteered, and Rick's lips rose in a half smile.

He reached out and took my hand, squeezing my knuckles. "I have to go back next week. The other pilots can't cover me for that long, especially not during winter. It's our busiest season." He sent a small smile my way. "I'll come back if I can—"

I cut off his words with a kiss, soft and slow, all-consuming. "You've done more than enough," I whispered against his lips. "We'll be okay. We'll come home to you as soon as we can."

"Home to me. I like that." He pulled back and cupped my face before kissing me softly, a slow peck that had me sighing. "I can't wait."

When we pulled apart, I saw Dad looking at us fondly and my face heated, I knew I'd be blushing like a freaking teenager. Who did that? I shook my head at myself. I was a grown man, apparently one who blushed. Even as a teenager I hadn't been embarrassed taking a boy home. My folks were cool, hadn't batted an eyelid when I came out. I'd planned it meticulously, writing out and memorizing a speech. Then when I had Mom, Dad, and Anna seated at the table eating breakfast, my palms got all sweaty and my heart started beating so fast I thought I was going to keel over.

But I'd worked myself up into a nervous wreck for nothing. When I blurted out that I was gay, Mom smiled, nodded, and asked me to pass the salt. Dad snatched two pieces of toast and took a massive bite of one, giving me a thumbs-up as he did, and Anna shrugged before reminding me it was my turn to do breakfast dishes.

But somehow introducing Mace and Rick to Dad felt a whole lot more significant than even my coming out did.

I watched Dad cleaning up the kitchen after a delicious pasta dish Rick and Mace had made, Mace wiping the little table down that we'd eaten on as Rick relaxed on the sofa next to me with a beer in his hand. Happiness swirled inside me. I didn't think I'd ever appreciate domesticity as much as I did at that moment. The people around me, my family, made my life wonderful. They'd lifted the burden and shared it, supporting me and loving me for no reason other than being me.

I realized that the people I'd surrounded myself with when I was on tour—who I thought were my friends—weren't even close to that. They were in it for how I could benefit them. These men before me, they wanted to give, not take. And my little girl with her precious eyes on me was adoring.

The whole afternoon had been blissfully domestic. I had no idea how much I wanted it until I'd experienced it firsthand. Even when we were on vacations it hadn't been like this—perhaps because the three of us were still hiding in one way or another. Now that the cards were on the table and we all knew exactly what we wanted, we wouldn't settle for anything less.

But before we could move on, there was something I needed to do.

"Rick, you think you and Mace could move Gracie's cot into our bedroom for me? I wanna put her down in there after this feed."

He looked a little skeptical, one eyebrow hiking up a little higher than the other for a moment, but he nodded nevertheless and began to stand. "Sure. I'll go do it now."

I grasped his wrist as he was stepping past me. "Not for the whole night, just a few hours. I need to get into Anna's room."

Leaning down to kiss me, he responded, "Anything for you," and I couldn't help my dreamy smile in return. I was so gone for him. For both of them.

Mace sat on the armrest of the sofa, massaging my shoulders with strong fingers. "Everything okay?" I leaned into his touch, sighing and smiling up at him just as Gracie finished the last of her formula. Burping her after she'd fed was a process, and it took a hell of a lot longer than I'd ever imagined, but since she'd had the first doses of medicine, she was a totally different baby. It killed me now knowing she was in pain and I hadn't done anything about it, thinking it was just a difficult stage she was going through. My instincts were off then, but now that I knew what happy Gracie was like, it wouldn't happen again.

Rick came back a moment later and began rubbing the bigger man's shoulders. I set Gracie on her play mat and watched my men press their lips together in a soft kiss. "I think I'm ready to look through some of Anna's things," I told them. "I was hoping you could help me do it, maybe just sit with me while I box it up for Goodwill or whatever. You too, Dad, if you're up to it," I finished, turning to him.

He hesitated. "I don't know, Caden. Today's been good, but…." He closed his eyes and looked up, gritting his teeth. I could see the internal fight he was waging, but he was being too hard on himself. It was insensitive of me to have asked, but I didn't want to exclude Dad either. He needed this as much as me—he was still mourning too. I also wanted him to get past his grief so he could function again. One of the things we'd done that afternoon was book an appointment with the Army's grief counselor. We had regular sessions locked in starting the next day; hopefully we'd be able to continue with them once we moved.

"Dad, I thought we could maybe do her shoes. If either of us feel like doing more, we can, but that's all I was going to start with."

Relief crossed his features and he smiled tentatively at me before giving me a single nod. I schooled my features and nodded back, but inside I was bouncing around, dancing with joy and nerves all at the same time. Dad had come forward in leaps and bounds in the space of an afternoon. It'd been such a shock to see him so present that I was a little paranoid he was going to crash again. He'd zoned out a couple of times but snapped back quickly, rejoining the conversation after a moment.

We did our new routine with Gracie before I put her in her crib, each of us kissing her forehead and whispering good-night messages meant just for her ears. I always told her how much I loved her. She was the light of my life, appearing during my darkest hour. I'd cherish her every day.

Stepping into Anna's room without Gracie's cot was uncomfortable. It was like I was intruding in my sister's space, especially because I was going in there to go through her stuff. Mace's hand on my shoulder encouraged me to go forward, but Dad opening the door to the built-in closet had me stopping in my tracks. Every item in there screamed Anna, from her engineering boots to the purple satin robe with feathers around the wrists. I sucked in a breath, knowing it was going to be harder than I'd ever imagined.

I kneeled down, pulled out a few pairs of shoes from the floor of her perfectly organized closet and handed them to Dad. I could hear the rustling of the trash bag as they were placed in there ready to be donated, but I couldn't look. Reality hit me full force, and I took a heaving breath as I fought off tears.

Within an instant, Rick's arms were around me, pulling me close while I clutched him. "I've got you, baby," he soothed.

"Jesus, even doing this is hard." I took a breath and pulled away from Rick, but he didn't let go, holding my hips loosely as I reached for the next pair. It was as if his strength seeped into me, and I managed to get through the rest without turning into a blubbering mess.

The floor of the closet was clear except for the row of shoe boxes she had sitting under the shoes at the back. The third one I lifted out was full, as were the next two. I eyed them speculatively. Did I want to know what was in there? Sooner or later I had to find out, and the warmth of being surrounded by family gave me the guts to open one of them.

It was a box of old CDs, and recognizing the cover of the one on top, I couldn't help my huff of laughter and watery eyes. It was one she'd given me as a teenager after I'd come out to her.

"Caden, you need to be a good gay man. Mack, from school, told me that all queens know the divas. He said it's basic factual knowledge, like douching, whatever that is." She grinned wickedly, snatched the new Foo Fighters CD I'd been holding and dropped the two cases on the counter. *"He's paying for both."*

"She made me buy this. Told me I needed to know my divas after I came out." I closed the lid, taking it and the two other boxes into the living room where I put the CD into the laptop and hit Play.

With Beyoncé belting it out in the background, I sat down on the sofa and opened the boxes again. Mace and Rick bracketed me, sitting close as I pulled the next CD out. Dad laughed when I handed him the burnt disc with a handwritten label on the case. "Breakup songs for the rat bastard" was the world's tackiest mixed tape. It was full of "I am Woman" songs mixed with a few power ballads that Anna played religiously throughout most of her teen years. Thing was, she was the one getting bored with the dudes and breaking up with them. She didn't need cheering up—she was the heartbreaker. It didn't matter though, because after every breakup she and Mom would crank up the music, eat a tub of Ben and Jerry's, and paint their nails. After my sister joined the Army, she continued to do that with Mom, then shot shit to pieces on the firing range.

Every CD told a story, and I shared how we used to dance around and be stupid, how we'd listen to them on repeat while we were playing video games, Anna usually kicking my ass every time. Ironically, the only ones I was better at than her were the shoot-'em-up games.

I loved those times. They were simple, fun. She was my best friend, the only person who knew everything about me. When I'd gone pro, she was the one I'd shared my hopes and dreams for the future with.

God, I missed her so much.

The next box had photos in it from when we were little, me as a toddler and her as a baby, right through to us starting school, and the third box held our school years. Typical Anna—not only put away but organized to within an inch of its life.

Dad picked up one of the photos and fingered it lightly, a sad smile on his face. "This was our first picture together. She was so much like Gracie, a joy." He blinked back tears and picked up a handful of others, smiling as he looked through them and passed each to us. He stalled when he reached the third photo, his breath catching and tears falling down his face. "Your mom was exhausted, but she still looked beautiful. She was sick when Anna was born, had this terrible cold, and Anna's birth wasn't easy. Fifteen hours of excruciating pain. But Pat soldiered on, never once complaining. I'll never forget that she shocked the shit out of her doctor. He was this kindly old fellow, like Santa except in scrubs, and the old man didn't have a clue how to respond." He smiled and shook his head.

"What did she tell him?" Mace asked.

Dad laughed. "She told me that we were done, finished. She threatened to cut my dick off if I even *thought* about having more kids, never mind suggesting it to her." He ran his fingers over the photo in his hands. "She wasn't even strong enough to hold Anna by the time the nurse set her in Pat's arms. I was supporting her so that she could cuddle her."

He passed the photo to me, and Rick's arms tightened around me when I looked at it. Mom was clearly exhausted, but she radiated this serenity too. In her arms was Anna. Dad was right, Gracie looked so much like her mom, so sweet and perfect.

But out of the three of them in that photo, it was

Dad who held my attention. The look of sheer adoration he was giving his two ladies said everything about why he was destroyed now. From the moment I was born, I was his little mate. His buddy. As a kid, I followed him around everywhere. But in his mind, Mom and Annalise were his goddesses, and he doted on them accordingly. He lived for the three of us, worked long days to come home and spend every waking moment living and laughing with us.

It was the first time I'd let myself think about Mom or Anna for any length of time. Remembering them was too painful, too raw. But it was different sitting there on the sofa together. Laughter mixed with mine and Dad's tears, and by the end of the second box, I was emotionally drained, but better than I had been in months.

"I'm gonna head outside for some air." I stood and headed to the front door. Letting it click softly closed behind me, I sat on the front steps and looked up to the night sky, stars twinkling overhead. "Love you, Mom, Anna," I whispered. The cool ocean breeze washed over me as I listened to the crickets and, farther away, the traffic noise from the freeway.

"Want some company?" Mace asked as he and Rick stepped out. When I nodded and shifted into the middle of the step, they sat down on either side of me. Mace pulled me close and kissed my temple. "How are you doing?"

I smiled up at him. "I'm okay. Better now that we've started out like this. I've got so many great memories of Mom and Anna, but they get pushed aside by the pain of losing them. They were incredible women."

Our conversation drifted off and we became quiet, each of us caught in our own thoughts. I was filled with a sense of peace.

"You know what I can't figure out?" Mace asked out of the blue, continuing before either Rick or I could answer. "Why did the landlord fix up so much of the house—the new steps, the siding, the windows. There's so much that's brand new, but you said it hadn't been up for sale. What was the point of spending all the time and money fixing it?"

I laughed but it held no humor. Anna had been asking for things to be fixed up from the moment she moved in, but even though promises were made, nothing had been done. "Landlord didn't do any of this. The whole place was crumbling before I got here. I did it all in the week before Gracie was born."

"You did it?" Mace's question held only curiosity. "How?"

I shrugged. "The stairs were rotting, so I pulled them apart to see how they were put together, then bought new lumber and mimicked it. It's pretty rough, but it does the trick."

Mace snorted and Rick shook his head, adding, "I can't believe I forgot that. We talked about what needed to be done, didn't we? Caden, this isn't rough, this is natural talent. If you can pull apart a set of stairs and copy them, you've got skills."

"I always wanted to work with my hands," I mused, running my fingers over the rounded edge of the step in front of me. "Maybe there'll be some jobs in construction I could do without training."

"My brother's friend owns a construction company," Rick chipped in. "He and Angelo have been friends for years. I could ask him to put in a call for you when you're ready to start working again."

I gaped at Rick. He surprised me every day, but I shouldn't have been. He was a treasure, far better than what I deserved. Excitement pulsed through me at the thought of getting to work with my hands every day. No, it wasn't excitement. It was hope.

"That'd be a dream come true." I didn't want to be outside anymore. I wanted to show both of them how much their support meant. "Come on, let's head inside." I grinned at them and reached for their hands, tugging both to their feet.

Screw it.

I pulled Rick to me and pressed my lips to his,

demanding entry. There was no slow burn to this kiss —it sparked and ignited a wildfire. Teeth clicked and tongues dueled as we devoured one another. When we broke apart for air, Mace traced his lips up my throat, and I turned into his touch, greedily sucking on his tongue. His moan was rough and deep, torn from his chest.

We fumbled, tripping over each other to get inside. Dad had gone to bed, and I was thankful he wasn't bearing witness to me lustily dragging my men through the house. We made it halfway through the darkened living room when Gracie's cry broke through the silence. I groaned, then felt instantly guilty for my outburst.

"Hey, stop that," Rick chastised me. "Don't feel guilty for hating bad timing. You don't love her any less. You're an amazing father." He squeezed my hand.

"You two go to bed. I'll join you soon," I assured them, detouring into Gracie's room. Picking my baby girl up from her cot, I smiled. The love I had for her was fierce, and my rekindled hope bloomed brighter as I looked into her eyes. I understood the look on Dad's face in that photograph, the love and purest of joy he'd experienced watching us grow up. I was experiencing it too.

I wiped away Gracie's tears with my thumb and

kissed her forehead. I wished my sister could've been the one doing it, but I knew how blessed I was. To have the privilege of being my precious daughter's first love meant the world to me.

"I love you, Gracie," I whispered. "Daddy will fix everything."

CHAPTER 12
CADEN

The week passed by fast and Rick had to leave too soon. Waiting in the airport lounge for his flight to be called, with a bunch of strangers around us, had me thinking that our seeing him off might not have been the smartest idea. There was no way I was letting him go without saying a proper goodbye, and Mace wanted to do the same. How the hell were we going to do that without shocking the shit out of the other passengers? Not that I cared what they thought, but still, why ask for trouble?

My leg was bouncing and I was wringing my hands.

"What's wrong, baby?" Rick asked me, resting his hand on my knee. Even that simple touch was enough to settle me.

"How are we gonna say goodbye with all these people around?"

"I don't give a fuck what people think," he said before leaning in and brushing his lips against mine. "I'll kiss my men goodbye, and then I'll kiss my baby girl goodbye too. If anyone has a problem with it, well, it's their problem. They can look away."

I grinned, knocking into his shoulder with my own. Warmth bloomed in my chest. "You called Gracie your baby girl. You really want that?"

He grasped my hand and lifted it to his lips, kissing my knuckles. "I do." He smiled shyly. "What do you want her to call you?"

I shrugged, then remembered my dream. "Daddy?"

"When she learns to talk, do you think maybe she could call me *papa*?"

I smiled. "Will you teach her to speak Italian?" He nodded and I grinned, leaning in to kiss him. I sobered quickly. "I don't want you to go. It's killing me knowing you're gonna be by yourself."

"Mace wants to help. Let him, please. It'll make me feel better knowing you've got the support you need to come home quicker."

"It'll make me feel better too," Mace added, wrapping an arm around Rick and nuzzling his temple. The lingering kiss he placed there showed me just how much he was struggling. "But C's right. It sucks that we'll be separated."

The boarding call came and went, and most of the lounge cleared out. There were only a few remaining families left saying goodbye to relatives. When Rick stood, Mace and I followed and the three of us hugged in a tight embrace. I breathed in his naturally spicy scent, wanting to imprint everything about him into my brain.

His hand tightened on my shirt, and suddenly holding him wasn't enough. I kissed him, long and slow, trying to tell him everything in my heart, but I needed to say the words too, needed to tell him exactly what he meant to me.

"You came when I needed you most. You've given me so much." I shook my head. How did I tell him he gave me my hope back? "I love you."

"And I love you." He nuzzled my nose and brushed a kiss over my lips. "I'd never not come to you."

Turning to Mace, he kissed him too, earning a few gasps from around us. "I love you too, Mace. Come home soon, yes?"

"As soon as we can." Mace nodded and ran his fingers through Rick's thick hair before pulling him close again and whispering, "Love you too." They kissed again, and a soft moan left my lips. God, they were beautiful together.

I kissed along Rick's jaw and earned a few more murmurs from the people left in the lounge. I tried to block it out, but when I heard the word "faggot" from a woman standing next to us, I couldn't ignore it anymore. Maybe I was being childish, but my first reaction was to give her a one-fingered salute. *Ignorant cow.* She muttered something and walked past, and I went back to kissing Rick and Mace.

At the announcement of the last boarding call, Rick pulled away and leaned down to Gracie in her stroller, kissing her softly on the forehead. He whispered something to her and stood, picking up his backpack.

Mace hugged me close as Rick walked backward toward the gate. "See you soon." He smiled at both of us and turned away quickly, heading for his flight.

We watched until the plane taxied away. As it did, Gracie woke up and cried her little heart out. Cuddling her close, I wanted to do the same. A piece of me was missing, gone with Rick, but it gave me renewed purpose and a sense of urgency. The sooner he was back in our arms, the better.

"Let's get back to the house. I've got some packing to do."

I changed Gracie, strapped her into her car seat and gave her the bottle while Mace drove George the Jeep home. The first thing I noticed when we got there was Dad sitting on the bench underneath the big tree in the yard. My heart sank seeing him there. I hated that I couldn't help him get better, and so far, the grief counseling we were attending was hard-going.

"Hey, Dad," I ventured tentatively. "You okay?"

He handed me his phone, an email on the screen. From what I could gather from a quick scan of it, it detailed an offer on his boat. He'd spoken to the harbormaster the day after we'd decided to make the move, telling him the boat was now for sale and as soon as it was gone, he wouldn't need the mooring anymore.

"Apparently someone wants it. The offer is really low though. It's going to take some haggling to get the price to a point where I can accept it." Dad's voice was flat. I was torn—happy that it might've sold, but worried about Dad. Pushing down my selfish desire to be with both Rick and Mace, I let him continue. "It's real now, you know? The boat going…."

"Are you reconsidering, Dad? We can work things out if you are. I don't want you to feel pressured." Mace and I shared a look. He'd paled as much as I was sure I had, anxiety knocking around in my chest.

"No, I want this. I think it'll be good to have a change of scenery. It's a little overwhelming getting an offer so quickly, that's all."

Mace sat beside him and patted Dad on the shoulder. "Queenstown is beautiful. There's this lake there, and the fishing is so damn good."

Dad smiled, and I dropped a kiss on Mace's head as he motioned for me to hand Gracie to him. I sat on the other side of Dad while Mace painted a picture of rolling white-capped mountains, crystalline skies, green pastures and a blue lake that had the township nestled on its shores. It really was the perfect place.

MASON

September

"THIS ONE. THIS IS IT." I DROPPED THE SIDE OF THE COT we were looking at in the baby store. It was easy enough to work, and the white would go perfectly with the other furniture we'd already picked up—a purple bookshelf, toy box, a fluffy rug and a white set of drawers.

"Hey, look at this," Ricky pointed out. "It converts into a tent when the sides come off and it's being used as a bed." Sure enough, Gracie would be able to have a tent attached to the top of her little bed when she was big enough to no longer need the sides of her cot.

I grinned and nodded, imagining purple flags and pillows littering the bedroom with the beautiful view of the mountain beyond the picture windows. "Hell yeah."

We called over the sales attendant and paid at the counter. It'd been a busy few days since I'd flown back into New Zealand. After not seeing Ricky for nearly two months, being in his arms after so long was indescribable, but just like every time Caden and I came together, there was someone missing. It was a waiting game now until he was with us again. Gracie's adoption had been signed off while I was in the air, traveling to Queenstown to collect my permanent residence visa. Now Caden just needed Gracie's passport and they'd be on their way.

They were coming home—well, to Ricky's house anyway.

Funny that, the idea of home. On paper I had nothing here, and yet I had everything. The man standing next to me, who'd excitedly shared with me his plan to decorate Gracie's room as we were driving from the airport to his house, and the one half a world away who was coming to us as quickly as he could. He and our baby girl were on their way, and I couldn't wait.

Before I left, Caden, Gracie, and I were sharing a room, and Gabe had the other one in the tiny apartment they'd rented. Caden had been ruthless, culling anything he didn't need to take from the house, and yet the apartment was still full of boxes. He'd sent his sister's things to Queenstown early so they'd be out of the way, and more boxes were yet to arrive.

By the time I'd flown into Queenstown, Ricky had emptied out the bedroom I'd stayed in and was converting it to Gracie's room. Light and breezy, it had a Juliet balcony overlooking the soaring mountains peaked with snow. When Ricky showed me the empty room, I instantly pictured it as a nursery. Moving to the double doors, I was captivated by the clouds gathering over the ranges, filtering the sunlight. We watched as the beams of light struggled to pierce the clouds, losing the battle as the evening rains began. There was an innocent romance in watching the fat drops fall from the sky: Ricky and I cocooned in the warmth of the dry bedroom. Standing in his embrace, I basked in his affection, his strong arms wrapped around my waist and his head on my shoulder.

All the items would be delivered the next day, so we walked out of the overly warm store and into the cool spring breeze hand in hand. We were meeting Ricky's brother, Angelo, across the street for lunch and I was suddenly nervous. Sweaty palms must have given me away, because my man squeezed my hand when we crossed the threshold into the cafe.

Taking a breath, I looked around, not that I knew who I was looking for. It didn't take long to spot him though; Angelo was unmistakable. He looked just like Ricky—dark hair swept back in a perfect coif and the same smiling whiskey-colored eyes as his brother—but he was very different too. Unlike Ricky, he had a slimmer build and was at least as tall as me. He wore black-framed glasses, suspenders and a bowtie, the epitome of a hot nerd. Another man was sprawled out beside him, his arm along the back of the booth they were sitting in, wearing a tight white tee with a leather jacket tossed haphazardly on the chair next to him.

"Hey, guys," Ricky greeted them after we'd ordered, sliding into the booth and motioning for me to do the same. "This is Mason. Mason, Angelo, and Trent."

Angelo eyed me up and down, and I swallowed,

waiting for him to finish his scrutiny. When he cracked a grin, every muscle in me relaxed. Family was everything to Ricky, and I was pretty sure I'd just passed the first test. Sure, I'd met the rest of Ricky's family—his mom, dad, and sister—over Christmas in Italy the year before, but that was different since we weren't together then. Now we were, and Angelo's opinion mattered.

"Hi, Mason." Angelo's Italian accent rolled the words off his tongue, and I marveled at how different he and his brother sounded. Where Ricky's voice was deep and smooth, reminding me of thick caramel, Angelo's was more melodic, a little higher in its register, but still sexy with that accent. He half stood, holding out his hand to me, and I eagerly grasped it, smiling at him. His eyes danced with mirth when he said, serious as a heart attack, "So… Rick tells me you're double-teaming my brother."

Still halfway into the booth, I hovered there, frozen. As if I were a cartoon character, my jaw dropped open and I stared at him, speechless. I could just imagine big "WTF" signs popping up instead of my eyes. I had no idea what to say, was at a total loss on how to act. He was yanking my chain, surely. But he was so damn serious.

Fuck me!

I closed my mouth, then opened it again to say

something, but nothing came out. How the hell did someone respond to that?

Ricky's laugh had me turning to him, and the heated look he gave me had my face warming. "Leave him alone, Angelo, you smartass." Tugging on my shirtsleeve, Ricky pulled me into the seat. "Come sit with me."

I slumped into the seat and let out a whooshing breath, making Angelo laugh and Ricky lean forward to punch him in the arm, adding, "You're a bastard, know that?"

Angelo gave us a saccharine smile, but his companion, Trent, was much more solemn. It took me a moment for the pieces to click into place—this Trent had to be the same man Ford worked with, the same homophobic bastard who'd nearly ended Reef and Ford's relationship before it'd begun. Hard to believe it now, because they were so solid—nothing could tear them apart—but in the beginning, Trent's interference had driven Reef away.

Why would Angelo do that? Why would he bring a man to meet his brother's boyfriend when he's so clearly against two men being together? I could only imagine his opinion on the three of us having a relationship.

Impressing Angelo became secondary. First, I needed to make sure Trent didn't stick his nose in and try to do some damage.

I assessed the man in front of me, meeting his gaze and holding it. Damn, the broody look worked for him. About Ricky's build, his dark hair was cut short, framing a strong nose and jawline. He had a natural-looking tan, but his eyes stood out most—almost black, they were fathoms deep. Soulful. Hard and judgmental at the moment. He hadn't said a word, but the scowl on his face was enough. I wasn't welcome in his presence, or maybe it was the fact that Ricky and I were being open about our relationship. Either way, I wasn't going to change for him, and I wasn't going to let him poison us.

"So, what's your problem?" I asked, raising an eyebrow at him. When he smirked, trying to hold back a laugh, I couldn't help my grin. It shattered the sudden tension I'd caused in the group, and Ricky visibly relaxed beside me.

Our coffees were delivered, a double espresso for Ricky and a long black for me. Trent flashed a smile at the waitress and it transformed him, making her swoon a little. I could only imagine how many women fell at his feet when he gave them that teasing look.

I shook my head and huffed out a laugh. He was a player—a bad boy player.

Feeling brave, or maybe recklessly trying to provoke Trent, I spoke to Angelo, replying to his earlier comment. "Your brother's too much for one man to handle. I need Caden to help me out with him."

"Oh my God, brain bleach." Angelo covered his ears and cringed while Ricky and I laughed and Trent smirked, then hid it quickly. He was a hard nut to crack, that one, but his slight nod left me confident that we might, one day, make it past average first impressions and glares. I hoped there was that chance—it'd be awkward not to get along with him, given how close Ricky was with his brother.

"So you're cool that there's three of us?" I hedged.

"Yeah." Angelo smiled. "I'm just glad that Rick finally managed to bag both of you. I've had months and months of 'Mason this' and 'Caden that.'" I squeezed Ricky's hand under the table, shooting a glance at him. He looked embarrassed at being called out, but hell, I was exactly the same. I'd talked Reef's and Ford's ears off about my two men without even realizing it. "I think he was struggling with the fact that there're two of you, but who the hell cares? I've said it before and I'll say it again: love is love and all that shit, and good sex is even better."

"Cheers to that." Ricky held up his mug and took a swallow, making desire rocket through me.

Goddamn. Watching him was the sexiest thing I'd ever seen. I wanted to lick his Adam's apple and keep going farther down, tasting him like I'd tasted Caden. Once I'd given my first blow job, I was hooked. Having that much power to send my man into the stratosphere was addictive, but I hadn't had the pleasure of doing the same to Ricky yet. I adjusted my half-hard dick as inconspicuously as I could and struggled to think of something else.

The conversation continued around me as I tried desperately to regain my focus. Something was being said about a memory from a few years back, but I wasn't taking in the words.

"How did you guys meet?" I asked, waving between Angelo and Trent, my voice a lot huskier than usual. I cleared my throat, but Ricky had heard it too and sucked in a breath, his body going rigid for a moment. God, it made me want to jump him. I cleared my throat and added, "Ricky said you've been friends for years."

Trent nodded. "I was watching the bungee jumpers from the bridge just out of town while Angelo did a photo shoot for them. I happened to be in the right spot at the right time—he asked for help with some of his equipment, so I hung around. That was, what, five years ago?" He turned to Angelo and his features softened just the slightest bit. They were obviously close. "We've been friends ever since."

"You going home this year, Rick?" Angelo asked,

changing the subject. Home to them was Santa Caterina di Valfurva in the north of Italy, the tiny ski village I'd visited the Christmas before. It was where we'd met Ricky, where the spark ignited when Caden and I had followed Reef there so he could be with Ford.

I would've loved to go back there; our Christmas was one I'd never forget. But dragging Gracie along for the two-day plane trip was a bit much, especially after she'd only just be getting used to Queenstown when we'd be preparing to travel again.

"I think it'd be good for us to settle in first, get some routine happening before we plan another big trip." Rick looked at me for confirmation, and when I nodded and smiled, he continued, "I'd love Mama to meet Gracie, but we've got next year."

"Is Caden really adopting her?" Angelo asked before he closed his eyes and shook his head. "Never mind, stupid question. Of course he's adopting her. Geez, it must've been hard to lose his sister like that." We both nodded, my heart breaking all over again knowing the anguish and utter devastation Annalise's death had wrought on Caden and his father. "He's lucky to have you guys."

Two hours later, after lunch, a few really good cups of joe and a lot of joking around, I'd realized two things. First, Angelo was great. He was charming and funny, mischievous, and he teased his brother endlessly. Second, Trent was a different man under the surface. He hadn't said much, but I'd seen him observe everything. From my conversations with Ford about him, I had the impression that he was an outspoken, ignorant fool. But the man in front of me was a whole lot more complex than that, one Angelo was fiercely protective of. Apparently that trait ran in the family.

I nudged Ricky. "Whaddya think about doing something when C gets here? Like a welcome party."

"How about everyone comes over to our house?" he asked without hesitation.

I know he continued talking, something about us cooking dinner and Gracie sleeping in her own bed, but my head was filled with a buzzing sound and my heart was overflowing. *Our house.* He'd called it ours, not his. I grasped his hand in mine and kissed his knuckles, wanting to wrap myself around him and never let go. That desire I'd been enveloped by earlier roared to life again, but this time it wasn't just being a horn bag—it was a need as intense as the sun to show Ricky how much his words meant, how much *he* meant.

"I love you," I blurted out. "You're amazing, exactly like Caden said. You'd do anything for us, wouldn't you?"

When he cupped my face, I leaned into his touch, needing to get closer to him, to feel his warmth. "Anything. Everything."

I shook my head, disbelieving that I'd managed to snag the most perfect of men to share with my best friend, the other love of my life. "Let's go home and pick which color we want to paint our baby girl's room."

"Angelo, Trent, I'll call you both and let you know when it's happening. It'll be in a few weeks."

"Make it a weeknight, yeah?" Angelo stated. "Wedding season's in full swing. I'm booked out Friday through Sunday until Christmas." He was a professional photographer, and while he did a bit of the touristy-type photos for local businesses and media outlets, his main specialty was weddings. His social media sites, which Ricky had shown me the night before, told the story of just how talented an eye he had.

Ricky bumped his fist and then did the same to Trent. Holding out my hand to Angelo and then his friend, I said, "It was great meeting you both."

"Yeah, you too, Mace. Look after him, okay."

Angelo nodded toward Ricky. "He's got a big heart, and I don't want to see him get hurt."

I'd been waiting for the protective brother to show his head. Honestly, if I had a sibling as close as these two were, I'd be saying the same thing.

I nodded, my tone stressing how serious I was as I proclaimed, "I love him, Angelo. Caden and Gracie too. They're everything to me." Then, embarrassed at gushing to two virtual strangers and my boyfriend, I ducked my head as heat flooded my face.

"We'll be in touch." Ricky nudged me and I slid out of the booth, waiting for him to do the same. His hand at the small of my back had me wanting to melt into him. I picked up my pace, dodging around the tables and chairs while Ricky's big body was pressed close to mine, kicking my lust into overdrive. As soon as we'd exited, he grasped my hand and dragged me along, and even with my longer legs I had trouble keeping up. He was a man on a mission, weaving between meandering pedestrians as we headed toward the parking lot.

I laughed when he saw an alley and ducked into it, cringing at the odor of the trash in the dumpsters. He groaned like he was in pain and pulled me out of there. "That smell.... No. Just no."

He shuddered and then, just as determined, led me along the street until we reached a mall. Cobblestoned walkways and soaring rough-hewn timber columns supported thick steel beams and a roof four floors high. Red brick walls and iron swing signs outside each of the shops gave the little space an industrial look, but the ivy growing along the walls made it cozy too, inviting. The sweet smells from the nearby cake shop helped draw me in.

I went willingly, pulling Ricky to me when he pushed me against the wall, the cold, rough surface a contrast to the heat of his body pressing into mine. His strong hands guided my face down to his, and he captured my mouth in a smoldering kiss. With eager lips and a teasing tongue, he held me in place, directing my movements.

I sighed and relaxed against him, giving in to him, and it just ramped our exchange up. Pushing his leg between mine, he started a slow grind, making me gasp as fire spread through my body, wanton need burning me from the inside. When his lips trailed along my throat down to my collarbone, I moaned out loud. His stubble against my skin, his firm lips and warm breath teasing me, torturing me in the best possible way had me arching into his touch, my hands spearing into his thick black hair and holding him against me.

"Want you, Mace," Ricky growled against the dip in my throat before he licked my Adam's apple. My hips bucked instinctively, my jean-clad erection grinding against his. I let out a choked gasp again, mindless with lust. My fingers tightened in his hair like they had a mind of their own as my ass clenched, begging to be filled with him. The puff of his breath with his chuckle told me he knew exactly what he did to me, but from the iron rod in his jeans pressed against my leg, he was just as affected.

"Ricky," I moaned quietly. "You need to take me home."

He growled, flat-out growled, and pulled back, fire in his eyes. "Fuck. Say that again."

"Take me home," I repeated. "Now."

His eyes closed and the blissed-out expression he wore was a heady aphrodisiac, but I didn't enjoy it for long. He pulled me forward again, lips slamming against mine as he kissed me like his life depended on it.

The ride back was quiet, but the air was electric, arcing between us. He pulled his 4x4 into the garage and jumped out, coming around to my side to open my door. He needn't have bothered—I was already out and striding toward him.

Grasping my hand again, he tugged me inside and straight upstairs to his bedroom—our bedroom—not stopping until we stood next to his bed. "Get undressed and lie down," he ordered.

"No." I shook my head slowly and trailed my hand down his body to the bulge in his jeans. Squeezing him and watching his eyes roll back in his head spurred me on. "I wanna taste you. Get C on the line. I want him with us."

I fell to my knees and unbuckled his belt, popping open the button and unzipping his fly. Before I could pull his jeans down, Ricky toed off his Chucks, his eyes on me the whole time. Biting back a moan, I hooked my fingers under his black Calvin's and dragged both them and his jeans down his powerful legs. The crisp dark hairs, the thickness of his muscles, the masculinity he exuded were all so new to me in a lover, but I didn't think I'd ever lose the shudder of anticipation that passed through me. Breathing his musk in, I ran my hands up his legs and watched as his dick pulsed, his semi quickly hardening again.

I blew a breath across his balls and licked him before sucking on the soft skin of his sac. I took one of his testicles into my mouth, the popping sound as I moved to the other lascivious. Trailing my tongue along the underside of his shaft, I licked along the veins from root to tip and finally got my true taste of him—salty and exotic, just like him.

His big hands on my head guided me but didn't push. I took more of him in, taking my time to work my way down his length, bathing him with my tongue and teasing him with barely there brushes of my teeth. Ricky's moan was heady, pushing me to go further, deeper. I wanted him to ride my face, to take what he wanted. I squeezed the firm cheeks of his ass, bringing him closer. Gagging a little, I pulled back, sucking breath through my nose, and Ricky took over, slowly thrusting his hips.

I ran my hand up his body, my fingers brushing against his lips. He sucked hard on them, making me mimic his move, and he let out a choked cry as precum flooded my mouth. My man liked it hard. I fingerfucked his mouth as I took him as deep as I could. Pulling my fingers free, I moved my hand to his ass and Ricky widened his stance. Brushing my fingers over his hole, I wet him, prodding gently like he and Caden had done to me countless times. I wanted to drive him wild, make him lose his shit and come all over my face.

My cock, throbbing in my jeans, was going to be permanently imprinted with the marks of my zipper. Tearing it open, I freed my dick from its confines. Ricky moaned when he saw me, and I slipped my finger into him. His entrance clenched tight around my first knuckle and I sucked harder on his cock, my other hand abandoning my own dick and moving to his balls. Rolling them in my hand, sucking hard and slowly inching farther into his passage had Ricky shouting out my name, his thick muscles trembling.

"Mason... oh God, Mace," he pleaded. My mouth full of him, I looked up and saw desire flaming in his eyes. "I want you to ride my face, *miele*."

It was all the invitation I needed. I pulled off him, slipping my fingers free, and scrambled to take off my clothes as he fumbled with the buttons of his shirt.

Finally naked, we stood before each other as I reached for the tablet he had sitting on the side table. We'd Skyped with Caden the night before as he was waking up. He'd be sound asleep now, but I needed him too. Dialing him, I set the tablet down where he'd be able to see the bed if he answered, then pushed Ricky down. Laughing, he reached out and pulled me on top of him, kissing me playfully. "Get back to sucking my cock, Mason."

"What's *miele* mean?" I breathed, wrapping my hand around his cock before kissing him again. Him thrusting into my fist and grinding against his hard length had a buzz starting in my body, but it wasn't enough. I wanted him inside me. I wanted his mouth on me. I wanted everything.

"Honey," he groaned, and I shuddered.

Pulling back, I swiveled around and climbed on his face, taking his cock deep in my mouth. Saliva dripped and I gathered it up, coating my finger before plunging it back inside him. Ricky tongued my hole, and my moan combined with the one from the speaker next to us.

"Fuck," Caden hissed, his sleepy voice wrapping around me as if I were in his arms. I knew I'd hit Ricky's prostate when he stiffened and cursed, his slit leaking precum onto my tongue.

My nerve endings were crackling, in rapture with the licking and prodding of Ricky's tongue. I was a slut for this—I couldn't get enough. As I shamelessly rode his face, he pressed deep, stretching me for his cock. I let out a cry, muffled by his shaft down my throat, my own cock pulsing between us. I wanted to be stuffed full, needed the burn of him sinking into me.

Pulling off him, I snagged the lube and condoms we'd stashed in the nightstand and yanked one out of the box, tossing it aside. Cool, wet fingers glided over my hole, teasing me, stretching me, and coating me inside and out. Tearing the condom open with my teeth, I rolled it down his length and held out my hand to Ricky. He drizzled lube into my outstretched palm and I slicked him up.

I was facing Ricky's feet, straddling his belly. In my desperation, I hadn't given a thought to how this would work.

"Mace, move down farther. Ride him like that," Caden begged. "But move the screen. I wanna see everything."

I reached out for the tablet, resting it on the bunched-up covers between Ricky's legs. I smiled at my love across the other side of the world, wishing he was close enough to hold.

"We wanted you with us," I explained, in no way sorry for waking him up.

Caden's response was to move his iPad down his body, showing me his cock driving into his fist. "I'm right there with you, Mace."

I moaned as my whole body coursed with desire. I lifted and slid down Ricky's body at the same time as he pulled himself up to sitting. Holding his cock in place with one hand, he held me steady with the other while I guided myself down. I struggled to stay relaxed—he was big. So. Fucking. Thick.

"Breathe, Mace," Caden directed. "Rick, fist his dick, play with his hole for me."

I moaned when Ricky did exactly what Caden asked, arching into his touch. Two thick fingers entered me and I gasped, rocking my hips as I rode him. But I needed more. I needed him.

Ricky pulled out and I sank down, his crown breaching me.

"Fuck, that's beautiful," Caden breathed.

Ricky rocked his hips and his cock slid farther into me, filling me more. I let my weight do some of the work, seating myself on him fully. The stretch, the fullness, it was overwhelming, but the pass of his shaft over my prostate had me seeing stars. I braced myself on Ricky's knees, swiveling my hips. His growl had me doing it again and again before he pulled me back against his chest. One hand splayed across my pec and the other on my dick, he pumped his hips and sent me into orbit. Hammering my prostate with every slow stroke, he took me to nirvana and my orgasm rocketed toward me. The buzz started low in my spine and radiated outward, my balls tightening and my cock throbbing as my blissed-out moans combined with Ricky's and Caden's.

I closed my eyes and imagined Caden's arms around me, holding me close like Ricky was. Their touch, their caresses, their warmth surrounding me both grounded me and lifted me high. Love and lust combined, detonating with the force of a nuclear bomb in my chest. I knew I'd never be the same again, and I didn't want to be.

I let go and flew, their love surrounding me as I erupted, my orgasm washing over me in waves. It was all-consuming. Heaven.

Panting, I started moving, trying to help Ricky

over the edge, but he held me tight, continuing his slow grind. His dick swelled in me and he emptied himself into the catch of the condom, his quiet cry into the nape of my neck the only noise to break the sounds of our breaths.

I opened my eyes. Caden had rolled onto his back, his cock softening after his orgasm. Ricky's soft kisses along my shoulders and the heat of his breath made me want to curl up against him, even though we were slippery with sweat.

He rolled me to the side, slowly pulling out and adjusting the tablet so I could see Caden again. "Baby, you okay?" he asked.

Caden's "Mmm" had me smiling. "I miss you guys."

"We miss you too," I whispered, the love and lust from a moment earlier mixing with yearning and the need to hold Caden close once more.

Ricky wrapped his arms around me and held me close, kissing everywhere he could reach. As we snuggled together, the warm spring day drawing to a close and the sun beginning to rise on Caden's end, we talked. We hadn't been together long, but it was long enough—I'd fallen for these men, and I didn't want to spend another minute apart from them.

CHAPTER 13
RICCARDO

Only a few more minutes, but damn, they'd been the longest minutes in world freaking history so far. A few more might actually kill me. Anticipation buzzed in my veins.

Waiting.

Waiting.

Waiting.

The plane had landed and people were meandering out, but there was still no glimpse of our travelers. I shuffled again, impatience burning far stronger than anticipation.

Where the hell are they?

Then I heard Gracie, her tiny cry growing louder as they came closer. I was vibrating, totally unable to stand still, but Mason kept me grounded, his hands on my hips holding me steady. Moments seemed to crawl by, excitement blooming inside me. Gabe was first through the doorway and he spotted us instantly, a tired smile lighting up his face as he wheeled two small suitcases over to us. Caden followed, a squirming Gracie in his arms, her back arching and her arms and legs kicking out. Her cries were angry, filled with frustration.

I clapped Gabe on the shoulder as I moved past him and over to Caden, reaching out to take Gracie from him. Our gaze connected and Caden let out a choked laugh, throwing himself into my arms. Holding both of them tight, I kissed my man hard, his touch, his scent invading my soul and burrowing deep. Not that he needed help getting there; he and Mason were already firmly imprinted on me.

Mason joined us and reached for Gracie, taking her from between our two bodies. I couldn't have been more grateful to him. Knowing how much I needed this and being willing to wait to say his own hello meant everything. But the man I was holding, the one clutching me like I was his lifeline, and who I was clinging to desperately as well, was all I could concentrate on. The warmth of Caden's lean body pressed against mine had me sighing in relief at the same time as a raw hunger swept through me. I wanted him, needed him closer. We were never going to be apart for so long again.

Breathing him in, I tightened my grip on him, sighing into his throat.

"God, I've missed you," Caden breathed.

"Me too." I kissed the warm skin under his ear, sending a shiver through him. His taste was intoxicating—a little salty, a little sweet and all Caden. I couldn't help sampling his skin again, kissing him slowly. "These last few months have felt like a lifetime. I can't believe you're in my arms." I rested my forehead against his. "But Mason has been missing you too. Say hello to him." I smiled, cupping his face. "And then we go home."

He closed his eyes, a smile tilting his lips. "Yeah, home sounds good." I pulled away but I couldn't let him go far, keeping my hand at the small of his back as he made his way to Mason. The love in my man's eyes as he held a giggling Gracie while he tickled her had butterflies taking flight in my belly. I was so damn lucky to be able to love these three people.

I took Gracie from Mason's arms and looked into her green eyes, marveling at how much she'd changed in a few months. Damn, I'd lost that time with her, missed seeing so many things. Never again. I wasn't missing any more. When she reached her little hand up and grabbed at my stubbled cheek, I grinned, hoping it meant she recognized me.

"Hi, *tesora*, I've missed you. You've grown so

big." I kissed her forehead and laughed when she put her open mouth against my cheek in a sloppy kiss, pulling away with the cutest face when my whiskers pricked at her lips. All the happy feels were sweeping through me; it was a high like no other.

I watched Mason and Caden together, wrapped around each other with their lips locked. Their kiss was passionate, desperate and hungry. They were rediscovering each other, and it was the most beautiful thing I'd ever seen.

Holding Gracie on my hip, I went to Gabe and embraced him, slapping him on the back. "It's good to see you guys here."

"It's good to finally be here. That flight was murder." He rubbed his face and smiled tiredly. "I can't wait to see the lake. Caden was telling me how there are rapids to go white water rafting on, as well as loads of fishing. Are you near it?"

"A few minutes' drive. Walking distance for sure. You looking at buying another boat?"

"When I eventually get set up, yeah, hopefully."

I reached out and squeezed Caden's shoulder as he and Mason broke apart but still held each other close. Motioning to the exit with my chin, I ran my free hand down Caden's back and smiled at Mason over the top of our man's head. We were finally together again. Best feeling in the world.

After picking up their luggage, we walked out of the airport together, watching the late afternoon sun sink behind the mountains towering around us. There was still snow on the peaks, but it would mostly melt in the next few months.

I couldn't wait for summer. This winter had been hard, not because of the weather—that had been pretty mild—but the distance, the yearning and separation from my guys had stretched it into a never-ending nightmare. Short days and long, dark, lonely nights. I knew Caden and Mason were together, comforting each other, and for that I was so grateful. But then Mason came to me, needing to get his visa sorted, and Caden was alone. The guilt that ate at me had me in a constant state of conflict—how could I enjoy being with Mason when Caden was alone? Every time we came together, I had them both in my mind.

Now, as the crisp spring breeze from the mountains washed over me, I looked over my family and was grateful for every day I'd had to wait. Because now it was all the sweeter. Even the view was better—and not just the one of two sexy-as-fuck men carrying a baby before me. Even the range was spectacular. Rolling peaks capped in white were a stunning contrast against the deep blue of the sky, only intensified by the snow. Puffy clouds floated on the breeze, the new season's grass viridescent.

We headed straight home, only a few minutes from the airport. Pulling up at the only set of lights between the two, I looked at my man in the rearview. Squashed between Gracie's car seat and his dad, Caden's exhausted smile was broad.

"Love you," I mouthed to him. When he said it back, I was left grinning like a damn fool.

"Rick, can I borrow your car tomorrow? I need to get Gracie some diapers and basically everything else." I could see Caden mentally ticking off the things he'd need for her. I just hoped the setup Mason and I had going on was good enough.

"Sure, no problem."

He smiled and nodded, closing his eyes as I started driving again.

Pulling up at the house a few minutes later, we piled out and headed in, Mason taking the baby girl he'd fallen head over heels in love with while I helped with the luggage. Delicious smells of tomato and oregano filled the air and reminded me how hungry I was. Mason and I had been cooking before we left for the airport, and Reef and Ford had brought over extras. We'd left the back door open so they could let themselves in, and I could hear them shuffling around in the kitchen.

"Oh hell yeah, that smells awesome," Caden moaned after breathing deep.

"Welcome home," Reef shouted from the kitchen before sticking his head around the corner and smiling at his friend. Arms open wide, he strode over and hugged Caden hard while Mason fist-bumped Ford and went on to introduce Gabe. Reef clapped Caden on the back, adding, "I'm so glad you're here, that you're staying."

"Me too," Caden replied. "It's a little surreal actually, knowing we aren't going back. This is our home base now." He grinned happily and my heart thudded in my chest.

"You'll love it." Reef smiled warmly. "And I'm so happy you gave that dumbass another chance." He motioned to Mason, grinning when my love narrowed his eyes playfully at him.

"How could I not?" Caden flashed a boyish grin at Mason, then aimed his happy laugh at me. "I love both of them."

My insides lit up and I couldn't help myself from reaching out for him. The butterflies in my gut had taken full flight, and my heart was doing flip-flops in my chest. I wanted to wrap him up and adore every inch of him until he knew the feeling was entirely mutual.

Taking him into my arms, I sighed at his warmth

and how he melted against me. He gripped me in a tight hug, leaving me with no doubt of his physical strength, but it was his inner core of steel that drew me in. His heart had been torn to shreds and yet was still filled with enough love that he could give it in spades. To Gracie, his dad and to Mason and me. Laying a soft kiss on his lips, I hugged him tight, never wanting to let him go, though I had to when Ford approached, wanting to greet the man in my arms.

"Happy to see you back here, mate," Ford said as he hugged Caden. "And Gracie is so damn cute. We'll sit for you guys anytime."

"She's pretty adorable, isn't she?" He smiled fondly at his baby girl, who was staring at Mason like he'd hung the moon for her. Mason was smitten too; the absolute adoration on his face said it all. I slipped in behind Caden, wrapping my arms around his waist as he continued to speak with Ford. He relaxed back in my arms and I sighed happily. "But she didn't like that flight. Cried for hours after we took off, then started again as soon as they started to lower altitude."

"Yeah, the change in pressure can be rough on kids' ears," Ford replied. They spoke more about feeding Gracie and the earplugs Caden had used until I couldn't wait any longer.

"Baby, can Mason and I show you something?" I dropped a kiss on his cheek, prickly against my lips from his five o'clock shadow. His smile made my heart hammer and his nod had me reaching for Mason, closing my hand around his. I motioned to the stairs, and he excused himself from the conversation with Ford before handing Gracie to Reef.

With Mason leading the way, we walked up toward the room we'd made Gracie's. Standing just outside the threshold, I was nervous—sweaty palms and my heart hammering I hedged, "If it's not okay, we can change anything and everything."

"What have you guys done?" Caden asked with a curious smile. Mason opened the door and stepped aside, letting Caden stick his head into the room. Painted mauve with white trim, the rich caramel-colored flooring that continued into the room gave it a warmth that only timber could. The old blinds had been replaced with white shutters, and purple gauzy curtains shone in the last of the evening's light. The bright purple rug sat on the floor over to the side of the room where we'd set up the reading corner, a nook bordered with the purple bookshelf and filled with matching throw cushions in white and silver. Gracie's cot and changing table were on the other side of the room, white furniture with purple linen for both. The white trunk of a tree painted on the wall was rooted in the reading corner, its branches spanning out along two sides of the room. Blossoms ranging from buds to full flowers covered the branches, and a kaleidoscope of butterflies of every color imaginable ran around the walls and over to the windows. Pictures of Gracie's family—her mom and her nan, as well as Caden and Gabe—hung off the branches.

Caden stepped through the door but didn't say a word. I held my breath as he took in every detail, his gaze wandering slowly along the walls, his fingertips tracing the white timber railing on the cot. His back to us, he let out a breath and his shoulders sagged. Disappointment surged through me. *Damn it, he hates it.* I shifted my gaze to Mace and he looked shattered, lips turned down and eyes sad.

"It's... I don't even know what to say." Caden blew out a breath and turned to us, his eyes glassy with unshed tears.

"Baby," I breathed, taking him into my arms, Mason cuddling him from behind. "I'm sorry."

He shook his head, pulling back from me. "No, I... it's perfect. I can't believe you did this, that you guys gave Gracie her own space. You've given her a home." He took a shuddering breath and clung to us, burying his face in my throat. Love, unrelenting and pure, washed over me as I held both my men tighter.

I had them in my arms, and I didn't care what it took, I'd fight to keep them there forever.

As if reading my thoughts, Caden whispered, "I never thought I'd be lucky enough to have you. Everything you do, it's... it's everything."

"We love you, baby," I murmured. "It's stupid how much." His puff of laughter brushed across my cheek, and I reached up to pull Mason's face down to mine.

I pressed my lips against his softly, a whisper of a promise. "I love both of you." I moved to Caden and took his mouth again, my tongue touching and tasting his. I captured his soft moan and pulled him closer to me, my other hand still at the back of Mason's neck, kneading the flexing muscles there.

I tried to ignore the throat being cleared in the background, but when it came louder a second time, together with a knock on the door, I pulled back just far enough to cast a glance sideways, Reef standing there smirking. "Your brother's here."

"He can wait."

"You want us to disappear for a few hours?" Reef was serious and it made me smile.

Caden's pupils were blown, his lips red and wet from my kiss. Mason's stare was heated, making me want to strip them both and worship every inch of their bodies. Damn, the offer was tempting, but I couldn't. My parents may have been horn dogs, but they'd taught me enough manners to know I needed to put the needs of my dick second.

"S'okay," I groaned, adjusting myself. "We'll be down in a minute."

I trailed my fingertips over Caden's cheek and smiled, pressing a chaste kiss to his lips.

My belly full after a huge dinner, we sat cuddling on the sofa together, our friends and family surrounding us. It was a picture I wanted to grow old seeing, happiness permeating every cell of my body.

"You should've seen his move." Angelo laughed. "Perfect going down the bowl, but on the curve up something went wrong and he lost it. Did the most awkward fall you've ever seen and face-planted in the snow. Total belly flop."

I was laughing so hard I snorted soda up my nose. Coughing and choking only made me laugh harder, my belly and cheeks hurting from the story. It was at Trent's expense, the poor guy blushing something fierce, but he was a good sport about it too.

"We could talk about the day you slipped on the green run, you know," Trent added, smirking.

"I was lugging around cameras and a bag of

lenses trying to take shots of a couple who'd just said their vows and wanted to run off to their honeymoon before I'd even had a chance to take any damn photos. Who does that? Leaves their photographer in the dust?" Angelo pouted playfully and I sighed, holding on to my belly as I wiped away the tears rolling down my cheeks.

Ford grinned, adding to the ribbing. "You grew up in a ski village. All you did during winter was ski and you *fell over* on a beginner run. That's pathetic."

Reef smirked at Mace and then at Caden before shaking his head at the rest of us. "You guys are amateurs—"

"Ah, hello," Angelo interrupted, laughing again. "We *are* amateurs."

"I remember when Reef was trying to master that backward five-forty and tail grab." Caden grinned at Reef. "There was a lot of eating snow then. Funny as fuck watching you fall out of the sky and slide down the slope."

"Getting winded totally harshed my buzz." Reef shook his head, laughing. "But you had a few good landings too, you know."

Caden nodded, smiling fondly. "I miss it—the snowboarding, not the competition."

"You do too, don't you, sweet?" Ford mused, pulling Reef close. Mason had done the same to

Caden, wrapping his arm around his shoulders and pressing a kiss to his temple while I took Caden's hand in mine, squeezing his fingers. The warmth of his grip, his presence had me smiling at him, happy that our friends were there celebrating his arrival, but wanting them to leave at the same time.

Gabe stood up and started collecting dessert bowls. We all followed, tidying up the table and dumping the dishes on the countertop.

"Just leave it all. I'll clean up later." I waved them away and tried to herd everyone out of the kitchen. It was getting late. I'd put Gracie to sleep a couple of hours ago and I could see Gabe fading, but more than anything I needed some alone and naked time with Mason and Caden.

Angelo got the message and placed a hand low on Trent's back. The other man stiffened infinitesimally but moved out of the room.

I ground my teeth together at his reaction. I hated that even though their friendship had lasted for years, Trent was still uncomfortable when my brother touched him.

"We're gonna head off, then," Angelo said awkwardly, his hands now stuffed in his pockets. "I'll speak to you tomorrow, Rick."

I nodded and flicked my eyes to Ford, who was

shaking his head at Trent. The other man was oblivious, his back to us as he put on his leather jacket.

"We'll leave you to it as well." Reef grasped Ford's hand and tugged him into his arms, whispering something in his ear. Ford blew out a breath and nodded.

"Thanks for coming, guys," Caden called, coming to stand between Mason and me at the front door. He reached out, hugging both of us close, and we wrapped him up between us.

Kissing his throat, I smiled when his breath hitched. I kicked the door closed, not waiting for our guests to leave before we went inside. A chuckle sounded behind us and I broke away, feeling guilty that Gabe had to witness his son getting it on with his boyfriends.

"I'm pretty tired, so I might head off to bed." He paused and smirked. "I'll be wearing headphones, so you'll need to keep an ear out for Gracie."

CADEN

I flushed with embarrassment when Dad walked away, laughing to himself. Then Mace grabbed me, lifting me off the ground, and I wrapped my legs around his waist. I looped my arms over his shoulders before grinning at him and leaned down to kiss his lips as he walked effortlessly up the stairs. He opened immediately, his tongue tangling with mine, moving together in a sensual dance. I broke away on a moan and Mace trailed his lips down my throat, sucking gently on the skin below my ear. A shudder passed through me and I clung tighter to him, his hard body pressing closer and rubbing me in all the right places.

The chub I'd been sporting from Rick teasing me kept filling until I was as hard as a fence paling. Shamelessly, I rubbed my cock against Mace's washboard abs. He massaged my ass, his fingers getting awfully close to my hole. I was primed, already on edge from a simple kiss—not that there was anything simple about Mace's kiss. Every time I touched either of them, it was like a lightning strike igniting a wildfire in me.

He lowered me to the bed, staying between my legs until we were both prone. Pressing his weight into me, Mace kissed me while Rick took off my Chucks and socks. Six thuds followed, each of our shoes falling to the floor, the sound so damn erotic. I dug my fingers into Mace's shoulders as he ground himself against every inch of my body. Rick straddled our legs and slid his hands under Mace's tee, his fingers pressing into the dips and curves of firm muscle as Mace arched into me, his breath catching. Rick quickly stripped off his shirt, and when Mace came back down onto me, I couldn't help but explore his broad body. Defined muscles quivered when I trailed my lips over them, tensed when I licked him and flat-out vibrated when I bit his pec.

Rick's grin was wolfish as he did the same to Mace's back. "*Miele*, lift those sexy hips of yours. I need you both naked." When Rick punched his hips forward, grinding himself against Mace's ass, the chain reaction had me moaning, my man's long, lean body pressing into mine. It nearly had me coming in my pants, but there was no way I was gonna miss this by firing off prematurely.

Strong hands wrapping around Mace's hips, Rick yanked him back and slid those deft digits around to undo Mace's jeans before tugging his clothing down. Mace on all fours, naked and hovering above me, had my mouth drying and my own attempts to shimmy out of my clothes stalling. Fuck me, he was gorgeous. Every inch of that body was sculpted from years of training as a pro athlete and then the intense coaching regimen he had with Reef. And damn, Rick and I reaped the benefits of all that hard work.

"You too, C. Take it off," Mace gasped, his hips stuttering forward as Rick shifted. I didn't know for sure, but it wasn't hard to guess that he was eating Mace out when Mace's eyes rolled back in his head and his breath caught. He arched his spine, pressing his ass firmly against Rick's mouth and widening his legs at the same time, moving so he was straddling me. I watched through heavy lids as he slowly jacked himself, adding a twist of his wrist over the head of his cock.

I was so fucking *hard*. Primed. I could come just from watching him touch himself, but I wanted friction, skin-on-skin contact. Yanking my jeans open, I sighed in blessed relief when the button fly was no longer uncomfortably pressing into my shaft. Desperate for friction on my throbbing cock, I pushed my jeans down over my hips, Rick tugging them the rest of the way down my legs and tossing them off the bed. I palmed my erection, hissing as the touch sent shards of sensation through me.

Rick's wicked mouth on my balls had my eyes rolling back in my head. *Goddamn, this is heaven, ecstasy.* His wet tongue slid around them and then up to my cock, swallowing me down. Precum leaked out of me, and he moaned as I pulsed inside his mouth. Jesus Christ, I was on the edge, ready to blow like Vesuvius.

There was an illicit pop that sounded when he moved back down to my ass, spreading me wider as he tongued my hole. Fuck, that little flick he gave me and the nips of his lips on my sensitized nerve endings were driving me insane, blowing my mind with every movement. I needed my men surrounding me, inside me, all over me. I wanted them to mark me, to claim me.

A growl left my throat at that thought—*mine*.

"I want you," I moaned, unsure of exactly what it was I was asking for. I needed to be closer, to reconnect with them in the most primal of ways. "I need you. Now."

"Fuck, yes," Mace ground out.

Rick was rolling a condom down my dick before Mace had even finished speaking. The *snick* of the cap on the bottle of lube Rick had somehow magicked up, the tight grip and the *schlick, schlick, schlick* of his fist sliding over me made me grunt like a fucking caveman. But then Mace shifted, the tight ring of his clenching muscle at the tip of my dick. Sweat had broken out all over my body, a bead running down my temple as I panted. I wanted in. I needed it. My body demanded that I slam into my man, claim him hard and fast; the last thread of my control stopping me was about to snap.

Rick wrapped his hand around the base of my cock as he guided Mace lower. It was like sinking into nirvana when his tight heat clamped down, strangling my dick.

But it was his eyes that had me racing toward the finish line. Pupils blown, pure and unadulterated need dripped from the intense stare of those beautiful hazels. I wanted this man with everything in me. I wanted both of them.

Mace sank down farther until the head of my cock had breached him, popping past the initial resistance. Breaths sawed in and out of my lungs as I fought off the call of Mother Nature herself—to fuck with wild, sweaty, orgasmic abandon.

I gripped his strong thighs, my muscles straining, shaking. "Mace," I hissed, begging him to move. He pressed down a little farther and I choked out a cry, my eyes drifting closed.

"Watch me, C," he growled, and I snapped my eyes back up to him.

Silky-smooth heat swallowed me, and that last thread of control I was holding onto snapped when his jaw went slack in utter bliss. He moaned, those pouty lips wet from the tongue he was gliding across them. He looked like he wanted to devour me whole, and I understood the dilemma entirely. My hips lifted of their own accord, Mother Nature laughing in the face of my inability to resist him. I surged forward until my pelvis connected with his ass, burying me deep inside him. My orgasm raced toward me, but I beat that bastard off with a stick; there was no fucking way this was ending before I'd made him scream my name.

Legs bent, feet planted on the bed, I thrust up into Mace. But I needed him closer too. Tugging on his neck, I brought him down to me, taking his mouth in a hungry kiss. We moved as one, giving and taking until I saw stars.

"Fuck, that's the most beautiful sight," Rick uttered reverently.

His beefy hands gripped my knees and spread them, and I lost my leverage to thrust. I choked out a frustrated cry that turned into a low moan as his tongue connected with my balls and Mace started riding me. Rick massaged my sac, lifting it out of the way as he moved to that sensitive stretch of skin above my hole. He had me arching into his touch, pressing my head back into the pillow and clenching my fists in a white-knuckled grip as he nipped at me. Mace lifted himself until only the tip of my cock was inside him, then slid back down my length in gloriously torturous slow motion. My heart was hammering so hard I was sure they could hear it, its *bump-bump* echoing through my head as I fought not to shout the house down.

Watching Mace, his plump lip between his teeth

and his skin flushed and slick with sweat, had me on the edge, nearly coming far too early. And then Rick breached me with one, then two fingers. I couldn't help my shout when he nailed my prostate, the fucker rubbing it as he gave me a wicked smirk. Mace slipped two fingers in my mouth and I sucked hard. I wasn't sure if the distraction was good or bad. Having any part of Mace in me was amazing, but it only had me thinking about his flushed cock leaving a sticky trail of precum on my belly with every rise and fall of his hips. I licked and sucked his digits, imagining I was cleaning the clear liquid off his cock while wishing it was the real deal inside my mouth.

When Rick pulled away, I groaned at the emptiness he left behind. Pushing Mace's fingers out of my mouth, I pulled his face down to mine and kissed him, sucking on his tongue and showing him just how desperate for them I was.

Mace moved back, gasping for air, and rasped out, "He's ready, Rick. Get inside him or neither of us'll last."

"Mmm" was Rick's only verbal response before he lined up his cock and rubbed it gently over my hole. When I cried out, my entire body vibrating with desire, he kneaded my thigh and murmured soothingly, "Let me in, baby. Breathe out and relax."

I forced my legs to fall open, widening myself to

him again and begging incoherently for him to push inside me. Hooking my legs over his arms, Rick lifted me to just the right angle and pressed home, his slicked dick popping past my resistance easily. The three of us were connected, one with each other, and it was sheer magnificence. He slid in deeper, filling me completely. I was stretched tight around him for the first time in far too long.

When Mace sank down on me, I was surrounded inside and out by them. *Holy fuck.* Sensation blasted through me, a shout getting caught in my throat.

They worked me over, loving on me until my pulse was screaming through my veins and my orgasm was like a dam ready to burst. I tugged Mace the small distance back to me, needing to touch every inch of him. My lips met his and he opened to my kiss without hesitation. Moaning, I closed my fingers over the hand he had wrapped around his cock and stroked with him. His channel grasped me tight, his body also teetering on the edge of the sweetest oblivion.

Mace's movements stuttered as I came, my orgasm crashing through me like a Florida thunderstorm. Surging waves of rapture fizzled through every nerve ending, every vein in my body. The noises I was making were incoherent as I pumped pulse after pulse of cum into the sheath between us. I grunted as another orgasmic shudder passed through me when Mace's ass clamped down and he emptied his load onto our chests.

My eyes popped open when Rick let loose a primal shout, albeit muffled, and Mace gasped, arching back. Rick, teeth bared, had latched onto Mace's shoulder and pressed his hips tight against my ass. He sighed in utter ecstasy, the grimace he wore misleading. I didn't think it was possible, but he swelled inside me, the pulses of his dick sending jolts through me as he came into the catch of the condom.

Breathing hard, Rick leaned his forehead on Mace's back and Mace rested his chest against mine. I was pinned, pressed into the sheets by their weight. It should've been suffocating, but it was warmth and safety and love. I'd missed them more than I ever thought possible. The whole time we were apart, all I'd wanted to do was pack my baby girl up and get on the next plane. Having them back in my arms, me in their bed, was like coming home and being shot to the moon all at the same time.

I wanted this forever.

My legs were like Jell-O and the rest of me was a sated puddle of goo. I had nothing left in me to even attempt moving, but it didn't matter. Mace looked after the condoms on both Rick and me, and my other man swiped a warm washcloth over me, then Mace. It was only a few moments later that they fell into bed on either side of me, rolling me so I was sprawled out over Mace, Rick spooning me from behind. Surrounded by them, all sweat-slicked hard muscle with the heady smell of man and sex in the air, I was floating on cloud nine. They held me tight while I relaxed into them, Mace's strong heartbeat against my cheek.

I couldn't help the smile that curved my lips. These two men and our baby girl fast asleep in the other room were my world. The three of them had lifted me from the depths of despair, pulled me out of the darkness and lit up my life like the rays of a new dawn did to the night sky. I would happily dedicate the rest of my life to their happiness, devote my entire being to loving them. With them, because of them, I had a chance at happiness and a life I could never have dreamed up.

My guys, strong, sweet and loving, had shown me with their every move just how far they'd go for me—literally to the other side of the world and back. They'd changed their entire lives to give my baby girl a home, and opened their arms to my dad, all to make me happy. To give me a home. Their arrival on my doorstep when I'd needed them most, when I was at my lowest point, was my lifeline. When everything was pushing me under, drowning me, they hauled me to safety. I'd lost my hope, but they helped me find it. I'd been sapped of every ounce of strength, and they'd loaned me theirs until mine returned.

Gracie was the only bright spark in my life, but then they appeared in an explosion of color, saturating my world of gray. They'd given me back my happiness, helped Dad find his way back and given him a fresh start. They'd gifted me with a chance to make something of my life, to make my daughter proud of her daddy. I was a little battered and bruised—Mom's and Anna's deaths would always leave a gaping void in me—but my family, my heart, were my everything.

They were all I'd ever need.

CHAPTER 14
CADEN

JUNE

Gracie sat between Mace and me on the chairlift, each of us holding her tight. She was adorable in her yellow snowsuit, booties, goggles, and beanie. I'd been holding out for the beginning of the snow season since I'd been in New Zealand, and even though it wasn't the first day of opening, it was the first time we'd made it up the mountain. Slipping into my own gear was like coming home, recapturing a piece of myself that I'd thought lost. When I was suspended, I didn't think I'd ever get back on a board again—that I'd even see snow again—but there I was looking out over the field of white before me.

I watched as a cloud floated high above us in the cerulean sky. The soaring peaks of the Remarkables rose up to touch the heavens, the blanket of thick white powder below beckoning us. The cold on my face and the sharp bite in my lungs gave me a jolt of excitement. I grinned, itching to get onto the slopes. I didn't even care that we were having to stick to the beginner runs, too nervous about trying anything trickier until I got used to carrying Gracie on my back. The carrier was already strapped in place on my shoulders, ready to hold Gracie when we got off the chairlift.

When my board touched the snow at the top of the lift, I pushed away, keeping the straps of the carrier against my shoulders. Mace had Gracie in his arms, and with Rick's help after he'd hopped off the chair following ours, he soon had her strapped in. I clicked my free foot into the bindings on my snowboard and swiveled around, finding my balance. The extra weight put me off a bit, but I could adjust for it.

"I think I'll be okay," I called out. "Can we try going down this way?" I pointed to the widest part of the field, one I could zigzag down slowly as I found my groove. Rick went first, making sure we had a clear run, and I followed close behind, with Mace bringing up the rear.

Those first few yards of sliding down the snow were transformative. A weight lifted off my shoulders and a smile split my face from ear to ear as childlike excitement pulsed through me. I wanted to holler and whoop; so I did. My enthusiasm set Gracie off and she giggled, squealing as I cut across the slope, turning us and reaching down to run my gloved fingers along the powdery surface. I could do this again, enjoy the snow for the fun times—I *was* doing it. There was no stress, no pressure. No driving need to prove myself. No, this was all about having a blast.

I laughed, carefree joy filtering through me as I changed the angle on my board and sped up. Catching up quickly with Rick, I called out to my baby girl, "Wave hello to *Papa*."

Gracie squealed gleefully as we passed him, but soon my guys were riding next to us again, never wanting to be too far away from the action. And Gracie was usually the center of that action. She was a little daredevil, the perfect mix of fearless and curious to keep three men on their toes. She was going to be a handful, but I couldn't wait. Life as it was right that moment was killer.

As I settled into the run, the wind in my face and snow rustling under my board, the super-soft powder floating around my knees, I was in heaven. Reef once told me that the mountain was his church, his place where everything made sense. Somewhere along the way, I'd lost my connection. It became my job rather than my calling, something I was so passionate about that I had to live it. That worshipping of Mother Nature by being on the slopes was a prayer I'd forgotten and had then evaded me for far too long. But now I had that connection back, and I was grasping it like a lifeline.

The weak winter sun, lacking in heat but still bright, the sky unmarred by pollutants, the pristine white of the ski field, the laughter, the love surrounding me lifted me once more. I couldn't believe it was my life. It was so magical, what I was destined for. Finding my own little spot in the world to live and love gave me peace, and despite all the action around me, a sense of tranquility settled over me like sinking into a warm tub. I had my family to thank for that—the three most important people in my world could take credit for all my happiness.

I grinned, holding out my fist for Gracie to bump. "You havin' fun, baby girl?"

"Yas," she called out in her sweet little voice. As the field began to level out, I slowed, already nearing the bottom of the run. Gracie grumbled, her eyes filled with disappointment. "Daddy, more?"

I chuckled. "Yep, we're going up again."

I looked up at the millions of stars blanketing the evening sky from my spot on the deck. The view of the darkened mountains in the background—the ones we'd skied for hours on earlier that day—and the sparkling heavens above were spectacular. It was a hella good snow season already; though it was only a week old, thick powder had already coated all the runs we'd shredded at the Remarkables.

More snow was forecast over the next day or two. It'd probably happen soon though, as the temperature was already dropping. The breeze was sharp on my skin, my breath fogging up the air before me. But I was cozy, wrapped in a coat and bracketed by Mace's and Rick's warmth. Rick's arm was around me and Mace's ran along the back of the sofa, his legs in my lap. I snuggled into them, sighing happily.

All day I'd been wanting to pinch myself. This was really my life. My guys sitting on either side of me and my friends, my family surrounding me—Gracie, Dad, Reef, Ford, Angelo and Trent. It was domesticated. It was love.

It was perfection.

I watched Dad with Gracie curled up on his lap, a blanket wrapped around her shoulders and a fluffy purple beanie on her head. Her dark hair curled up, framing her green eyes and heart-shaped mouth that was turned down in a pout as she waited impatiently for her s'more. With arms outstretched, she repeated, "More, more," to Angelo.

She was an angel, but that day had proved that a little of mine and a lot of her mother's blood ran through her veins. Fearless and strong-willed, she wouldn't let us leave the mountain until she'd had her fill. My sister's spirit lived on in her, and every time I looked at my baby girl on those slopes, I saw it in her eyes, the dancing light that told me Annalise was with her.

Exhausted, she'd crashed in the car on the way home and slept for hours, waking just in time for everyone to arrive. Fiercely independent and smart as a whip, she'd toddled down the stairs, refusing Rick's help, and greeted the men now sitting around the fire with us.

Our little girl had captured all our hearts—we lived for her giggles, and the older she got, the more they happened.

The four of us had found our groove. *Dada* was the best father figure I could ever have asked for; Mace was a teacher at heart, and she was blossoming from his tutelage. When she needed comfort, we were all right there, but it was *Papa* she always wanted, something I did too. Ricky was her wall of strength, the safety she sought when she was scared. I think I had the best role of all though.

Seeing Gracie as she closed her eyes at night, watching her get all cuddly and fall asleep, was the coolest thing ever. I treasured those little moments with her.

"More, more," Gracie huffed indignantly, a little V forming in her forehead. Uncle Angelo and Uncle Trent were taking far too long as far as she was concerned, but I could see why. They'd roasted the marshmallow, pressing it between the cookies, and were now waving it around, cooling it down so she didn't burn herself. My unofficial brother-in-law and his best friend doted over her too, as did virtually everyone else who met our baby girl.

I shook my head, smiling, and turned my attention back to the discussion about Reef's guest interview with a relative of Ford's. The guy was apparently an ex-TV star who was now an ambassador for an LGBTIQ organization in Australia. Reef had spoken to him about his experience as a pro athlete and having to hide his sexuality, what it was like coming out, and more recently how Gus and Adam, the two superstar Olympians, had inspired Reef and so many others. Reef had done a great job, and the passion he carried into his training and competition—the same passion that made him a world champion—was so apparent in the interview. It was clear that he loved his new gig as a ski instructor, and bookings for his lessons had tripled since he'd been on-air.

Teaching kids how to snowboard was the perfect job for him. I sometimes wondered if I could've held down something like that after I retired, but the what-ifs never lasted long. I loved my job. It was a lucky break getting hired on the construction crew, and I was proving my worth every day. Building called to me, and getting to work with my hands was the greatest, even if the winter mornings on site were fucking freezing. It was hard work, honest work. I'd come home sweaty and dirty, but I was making a difference, having a hand in creating something that would become a family's home, a place where they made memories every day.

The song playing softly in the background ended, and Charlie Puth's "One Call Away" started, filling the air between the laughter.

"Go on, you know you want to," Rick interjected.

Reef flashed a smile at Ford, who was looking at him like he was his world. He whispered something in his ear before they stood up. The smile on Ford's face, the love reflected in his eyes, would've made me swoon had I not been on the receiving end of the same love from Rick and Mace every day. Stepping around the birthday presents littering the deck, they moved down onto the grass and wrapped their arms around each other tight, swaying slowly to their song.

"Up?" Gracie asked sweetly, her face and fingers sticky with marshmallow and cookie crumbs from the s'more she'd just devoured. I snagged a wet wipe from the tub on the table and went to her, cleaning her up before popping her on my hip.

"You want to dance, baby girl?"

When Gracie nodded enthusiastically, I took the same route as Reef and Ford, moving down to the patch of grass in the yard. It didn't take long for Rick to step in front of me, taking my free hand in his and wrapping his other arm around my waist, keeping Gracie between us. Mace came in behind me, standing close and nuzzling into my neck just as the song wrapped up.

There was barely a pause before Ed Sheeran's "Perfect" started. With Ed crooning about a sweet girl who held his heart, I smiled at Gracie. She was my perfect girl. They were my perfect guys. Dancing there, under the night sky blanketed with millions of tiny pinpricks of light sparkling like diamonds, I looked up into the heavens. It was overwhelmingly beautiful, and in that moment I knew without a doubt that Anna had heard my begging. She was right there with us, loving us.

"Can you feel that, baby girl?" I took a shaky

breath, blinking back tears of joy. Knowing Anna could still see her daughter, could still watch over her and love her, had my heart exploding with joy. "Your mama's here. She's an angel watching over us."

Losing Anna had broken me, but from her loss, I'd gained a family. We were a perfect little unit of four. They were everything I needed but never in a million lifetimes would've dared dream possible.

Life was like that though, moments of sheer perfection in an ever-changing world. My journey had been tough so far, but with my family next to me, I knew I could face anything.

Though somehow, I knew clear skies laid ahead of us now.

THANK YOU SO MUCH FOR READING ALL HE NEEDS. IF you haven't done so already, please consider checking out IN SAFE ARMS.

ABOUT THE AUTHOR

By day Ann Grech used to live in the corporate world and could be found sitting behind a desk typing away at reports and papers or lecturing to a room full of students. She graduated with a PhD in 2016 and is now an over-qualified nerd. But the grind got old, and the voices got louder. She still has the librarian look nailed, but she's a little freer to be herself now.

She's never entirely fit in and loves escaping into a book—whether it's reading or writing one. But she's found her tribe and loves her book world family. She dislikes cooking, but loves eating, can't figure out technology, but is addicted to it, and her guilty pleasure is Byron Bay Cookies. Oh and shoes. And lingerie. And maybe handbags too. Well, if we're being honest, we'd probably have to add her library too given the state of her credit card every month (what can she say, she's a bookworm at heart)!

In 2019 she was an Award-Winning Finalist in the Fiction: LGBTQ category of the 2019 Best Book Awards sponsored by American Book Fest for her story *In Safe Arms*.

She also publishes her raunchier short stories under her pen name, Olive Hiscock.

Ann loves chatting to people online, so if you'd like to keep up with what she's got going on.

Join Ann's newsletter:
http://anngrech.us8.list-manage2.com/subscribe?u=0af7475c0791ed8f1466e7fd9&id=1cee9cdcb6

Join Ann's reader group: https://www.facebook.com/groups/1871698189780535/

Visit Ann's website for her current booklist:
www.anngrech.com

ACKNOWLEDGMENTS

This story wouldn't have happened without the help I received from so many beautiful people. To Susan Horsnell and Gibby Gibson, thank you both for helping me create Anna. Gibby, for your knowledge of all things military and picking the perfect career for a kickass woman, and Susan, for your medical knowledge and guidance. Anna's story shattered me. It was one of the hardest things I've ever written and Susan, your guidance in tweaking the medical parts of it was invaluable.

Another thank you also needs to go to my beautiful critique partner who looks at all my work and always sets me on the right path. Kariss, thank you, beautiful. I always appreciate your eyes. On that note, another thank you to Kristin for her mad editing skills (apologies for all the comma splices and unnecessary words!), Paula and Andrea for their beta review and Kim and Tina for their eyes. Becky, for your years of unwavering support and for giving me the chance to join the Hot Tree Publishing family, thank you, gorgeous. You know I adore you, right?

Thank you also to Tracey Weston for your stunning cover. As soon as I saw it, I knew it was perfect. You managed to capture everything Caden without even knowing him.

Caden's backstory came to me when I was literally in the middle of a sentence while teaching Sport Law and writing *Whitewash*. I completely lost track of what I was going to say and the rest is history. Thank you to those fifteen or so students who waited for me to reengage my brain and resume our chat about drugs, drug testing in sport, and the infamous cheaters. Caden had to be the bad guy in *Whitewash*, but I knew there was so much more to him and for a long time, he was begging me to tell it. He was never alone though—Rick and Mace were always right there with him, and Caden was pretty insistent that he wouldn't choose between them. So, Caden, thanks for butting heads with me and winning!

For my A-Team, who kept pushing for another installment in Reef and Ford's world, here it is. I hope that I've done Caden, Mace, and Ricky's story justice for you. Thank you always for your friendship, encouragement and mild outrage when I get up on my soapbox about something that's got me worked up! You're always there, and I appreciate you to no end for it.

Hubby, you always had the hug I needed when I

was crying over Caden. Thank you for not questioning my sanity too often, but poking fun of me was not nice. These guys are not just fictional characters. You should know that by now! B and J, you boys are so damn special to me—you and your dad are the loves of my life. Holding you in my arms for the first time were my two greatest moments. Thank you for choosing me as your mum and for giving me the inspiration to write about the love a parent has for their kids.

Last, but not least by any stretch of the imagination, a huge thank you to all the readers who pick up my books and the bloggers who show so much love for the book community. I can never thank you enough for your love and support over my years of writing. The time you take to buy, read, review, reach out and share your thoughts about my books is so very appreciated. Thank you for pushing me to be a better writer with every word I type.

Ann xx

ABOUT THE PUBLISHER

Hot Tree Publishing loves love. Publishing adult romantic fiction, HTPubs are all about diverse reads featuring heroes and heroines to swoon over. Since opening in 2015, HTPubs have published more than 300 titles across the wide and diverse range of romantic genres. If you're chasing a happily ever after in your favourite subgenre, HTPubs have you covered.

Interested in discovering more amazing reads brought to you by Hot Tree Publishing? Head over to the website for information:

WWW.HOTTREEPUBLISHING.COM

facebook.com/hottreepublishing
twitter.com/hottreepubs
instagram.com/hottreepublishing